Love Diseases

Olivia Scott

Contents

Chapter One

Blake Beckson was a disease of a human being.

I didn't have to know him to know that. I was walking behind him on our way to school; his actions along the way revealed how much of a tool he was.

He had his sunglasses on — even though it was only partly sunny — and those annoying pants with the elastic bands around the ankles. He was the visual manifestation of asshat.

"Excuse me?" he said, voice sickeningly sweet and directed at Nancy, the 90 year old woman who lived down the street. Nancy was struggling to drag her garbage can out to the bottom of the driveway, clearly vulnerable to evil men like Blake. "Can I help you with that?"

A trap, surely. Nancy, the gullible old lady, looked pleased and slightly surprised. "Oh...! Oh, thank you, young man! What a kind boy you are."

Blake waved his hand in the air flippantly, dismissing Nancy entirely. "Oh, don't worry about it! It's my pleasure."

He was Satan, quite frankly.

Rolling up his shirtsleeves, probably all for show, Blake approached Nancy. If it were a movie in the theatre, the Jaws theme song would've been playing in the background and the audience would be on the edge of their seats, clutching their buttery fists.

Blake grabbed Nancy's garbage can and, with ease, brought it over to the end of the driveway. Nancy, all smiles, gave him a hug and offered him cookies.

Blake declined.

...Only a monster would decline cookies.

Only men like Blake Beckson could take pleasure in one-upping old ladies by moving their garbage cans.

Only. Blake. Beckson.

And the fact that he clearly scoffed at the cookies she worked so hard to make?

Disgusting.

Satan incarnate began to whistle an upbeat tune, clearly some kind of Satanic spell, and walked down the road with a spring in his step. He was plotting something.

He was probably thinking of eating children's entrails.

I wouldn't be shocked.

It was about halfway to Lincoln South High School when Blake turned around.

"Hey, uh, Jake? I've noticed you've been kind of, um, following me? For the past twenty minutes? You know, I think it might be a lot less awkward if you walked with me and not, um, directly behind me."

How self-absorbed.

"I don't want to walk with you," I replied honestly, like the good person I was.

Blake awkwardly shuffled his feet and tugged at his coat sleeve. "Are you sure? I'd really like to walk with you. Maybe get to know you a bit? You're in my precalc class. I sit, like, two seats to your right."

"Listen, Blake," I said. "I don't like you. We've been over this."

Blake frowned. "Okay."

He looked sad that I didn't want to walk with him. He was such a deceptive person.

Up ahead, there was a man with a long walking stick and sunglasses on. It wasn't even sunny though. Clearly he was a dickbag just like Beckson.

It wasn't surprising in the least when the antagonist of everyone's story walked over to the man and linked arms with him.

"Are you trying to cross the street?" Nosy Beckson asked.

The man nodded. "But I can't tell if there are cars coming. My hearing ain't what it used to be."

Psh. Take your goddamn sunglasses off and look both ways, idiot.

Beckson's smile was maniacal. "I'll help you."

Sure enough, he crossed the street with the man and walked him all the way to the bus stop. The man sat down on the bench and patted Beckson's arm. "It's a good thing there are kids like you around. Thanks, kid."

The use of the word kid practically twice in a row was cringy.

Looks like he was an asshole too.

"It was no problem, sir," Beckson leered.

After a million years, we reached our destination and I wasted no time getting as far away from Blake Beckson as possible. He bounced over to his group of friends and I went to mine.

"I hate him," were the first words out of my mouth.

"Who, Blake? Dude, you really have to get over that hang up," Kay said. She looked up at me out of the corner of her eyes. "Just because your names rhyme doesn't give you a right to hate him."

"It pisses me off. People could confuse us! People do confuse us."

Kay glanced at Blake Beckson, the epitome of a sort-of-built, but still clearly a teen, seventeen year old white guy, and at me, a 6'3" track star clocking in at 245 lbs of muscle.

Okay, maybe nobody had ever confused us. Clearly I was way hotter than he was.

"Okay, fine. But don't forget about the automatic light outside his garage," I added.

"I highly doubt you get woken up by it," Kay snorted. "You're just looking for excuses because you don't want to tell me the real reason. Alright—oh, hey Ben!"

Ben. I liked Ben. Ben was good people.

Ben was the smallest human on planet earth also. He was a full head shorter than me.

I could just tuck him right under my chin and cuddle him. ...Not that I would do that. That would be weird.

"Oh, looks like I missed J's overcompensatingly angry, and yet still very clearly gay and in-love, speech about Blake the Bombshell. Awesome!" he laughed.

Ugh. Ben.

"It's not gay and in-love," I clarified. "If anything, my thought about holding you close and tucking you under my chin was gay and in-love. My feelings for Blake are filled with pure, unbridled hatred."

Kay snorted and nudged Ben. "Ha, it's almost like he believes that."

Ben blinked. "...Tuck me under your chin? Fuckin' what..."

I decided to ignore him and go inside. I needed to get as far away from disgusting little Blake Beckson as fast as humanly possible.

Besides, why would they ever think that I could have feelings for Blake? Love was practically a disease.

Chapter Two

I managed to lose Ben in the struggle of getting to my locker. The hallway was filled with a crowd of students shoving their way through as if their lives depended on it. I made my way to my locker and grabbed what I needed for statistics.

I found Ben again once I made it to the classroom. He gave me a grin and I plopped down beside him with a nod.

Ms. Nelson began to write problems on the board and I groaned. Ms. Nelson glared and called me rude. Oh well.

It was a long fifty minutes.

Ben spent all of statistics making small paper boats with his notebook paper, and the second the class was over he dumped them on my head.

Good thing everyone was busy grabbing their things and running like Satan, (or, I suppose, Blake Beckson) was behind them.

"Why." I looked mournfully at my lap, which now held a handful of pretty origami boats.

"I have an idea," Ben said.

"...But why."

"Listen to me Jake. I have a great idea. You know how you're like emotionally constipated and kind of awkward?" he asked me. He blinked.

Wow.

He had very long eyelashes.

"I suppose."

"And how you talk weird?"

"...Yes?"

"Well, I think I can help refine you so that you're the perfect gay boyfriend for Blake," Ben said. "I've been doing some research—"

"Oh God."

"—and I learned a little bit. I think I can be your wingman. Like, you know in those gay fanfics, with the obnoxious white girl who like oversteps boundaries and shit? That's me, 'cept I'm black and charming."

Wow, that was a lot to process. "Did you just come out as gay?"

"What, no—what the fuck, guy?"

"Well, you've done research on homosexuals and read stories about—"

"Alright, fuck off man, alright? Good. Back to your gay crush on Blake." Ben cracked his knuckles. "I pretty much got this shit down pat. You're like the top, right? Because you're all tall and strong and shit. And Blake is totally the bottom— isn't that like the uke? Yeah, so—"

Ah. No thank you. No, I didn't like this conversation. I grabbed my backpack and walked away.

"Jake, oh Jesus, slow down! Come back!"

Did people give us strange looks as I walked to class and Ben trailed behind me whining? Yes, they did. Including Blake, who was leaning up against his locker next to a girl.

Rude.

...The look was rude, not being near a girl. Being near a girl was totally fine. Cliché and typical straight guy of him, but still, you know, acceptable.

"Jaaaaake, come baaaaack!"

Ugh. Ben.

"Fine, what?" It was nice that we stopped next to my locker too, so I could pull out the books I needed for after my free period.

"I have a plan for your man!" Ben whispered. He even got up on his tippy toes to help himself out.

"You're so cute and small," I told him. He looked at me like I'd said the most offensive thing on Earth.

"Fuck you Jake, I'm trying to be a good friend here. Plus, so weird when you say stuff like that with no expression on your face. Listen to me—I'm gonna talk to Blake, yeah? I'm just gonna be like, 'Hey! Sorry my man hates you, how do you feel about him?' You know? Subtle."

"I don't like him," I said. "I don't. He represents all that is evil in this world."

"Has anyone told you that you're melodramatic? Jeez." He rolled his eyes and gave me a slightly impatient gesture once I'd packed up my books. "C'mon, big guy, we gotta find Kaylee. Let's move."

We found her standing next to her friend Christine by the vending machine, guzzling root beer. Christine was one of those really tall skinny girls that sort of intimidated me. She was probably what most assholes would call "fake" considering her layers of finely applied make up and her platinum blonde hair.

"I'm stressing out, Kay. Partial diff— oh, hey guys!"

"Hey Christi," Ben said. Ben was also the type of person who nicknamed. "You look like you're thinking about math."

"Yeah," Christine sighed like she was trying to expel her stress out of her body. "Calc sucks. But it'll all be worth it if I can pass the AP test and never have to take a math class in college."

"Here, here!" Kay said. She raised her soda and clinked it against Christine's. "We'll make it through together. What's up guys?"

Ben leaned in. "Jakey's hard dick for Blake Beckson, that's what's up. He wants to make Blake his catamite."

Kay made a meaningless gesture with her hands that communicated her utter confusion. "There goes our normal, pleasant conversation."

"What even is a catamite, Ben?" Christine asked, looking a little grossed out. "Just say uke."

"I think sex slave is more accurate," Kay pointed out.

"I'm leaving," I said. "I keep saying, I hate. Hate. Blake."

Wait. Lightbulb.

"I like someone else, actually," I confessed, after a pause. Well, maybe not confessed. It was a lie; I didn't like anyone.

"It's me, I knew it!" Ben yelled, catching the attention of some onlookers. "Jake, man, I love you like a brother, but not like a dick-up-the butthole kinda love. Maybe, mutual jack off session while drunk love? I feel like I could also probably kiss you and be cool. But, nope, I could never let you stick your dick up my ass."

"It's not you. You're too short."

"I hate you."

"I like someone else. He's in my English lll class. He's hot. Now, goodbye, I'm leaving."

This time they didn't stop me. They just stared after me, looking mystified.

—/—

"Can we please walk together?"

After a long and draining day at school, I literally had to blink twice before fully registering what was in front of me. Blake fucking Beckson, the boy who declines old lady's cookies and wears khaki joggers and stupid t-shirts.

Actually, right now he was in khaki joggers and a ratty grey sweatshirt. Which was worse.

"No."

I began my walk home without him. I usually aimed for a 10 foot difference in between us on our walks to and from school. However, I typically kept Blake in front of me so he couldn't stab me in the back.

Unfortunately, today would have to be different.

"Wait up!" Blake said. He jogged a little to catch up to me. "Can we, like, talk?"

"No."

"Why? I'm so confused. Your friend talked to me today. He said that you wanted to make me an, um, catamite? I don't know what that is, but—"

"Don't listen to Ben. Please don't google that. He's lying to you to get a rise out of me," I said.

"Huh. So, why do you hate me?" Blake asked. Blake was the proud owner of some creepy fucking green eyes. And the way his hair curled a little at the nape of his neck and by his temples?

... Actually, that was a little cute.

Shit, Ben was getting to me.

I decided to shake away my thoughts and answer the short male in front of me. "You are annoying to me. Especially the way you dress."

"Huh? Really?" He glanced down and grinned. "I mean I'm no fashionista, but I'm pretty sure grey is the new black right now."

"Not funny. Also, I was referencing the atrocity you call a pair of pants."

"Joggers? These are in. Everyone on Tumblr wears them! Not that I, like, go on Tumblr, but my girlfriend tells me that they do," Blake said, desperately trotting along to keep up with me.

I liked Tumblr.

Blake was so evil.

I sighed. I didn't think it would have to come to this. 'Blake. Blake. Blake the mistake—"

He blinked at me.

"—You have a girlfriend, which also bothers me. Not in the way Ben probably implied, but in the way that says, you know, I am repulsed by straight people."

"Hey, that's mean."

"Not all straight people — I like Kay — but straight people that wear joggers? Yeah. Gross. Listen, I have to go keep my usual distance from you. Goodbye."

Blake blinked at me again. "Wait. Wait for one second."

I decided, against all the logic in the world, to wait.

"Do people really call me Blake the mistake?"

I sighed... again. "Am I people?"

"...Yes?"

"Then yes, people do. Goodbye now, Beckson. See you tomorrow."

I wasn't quite at our houses yet, but it was okay. I walked a little bit faster and maintained the usual ten feet away rule. Well, maybe more like nine feet. Or eight. But that was fine, Blake wasn't as annoying when he was processing how irritating he was.

He was definitely irritating. And I did not, as Ben implied, want to make him my catamite.

Chapter Three

Just as a warning, there's insensitive language in this chapter.

When I opened my door to walk to school, Blake was on the other side. Standing on my porch. Wearing sunglasses, as usual.

As if trying to kill me.

Disturbing.

"Jake." He stared me dead in the eyes. Through his sunglasses.

"Yes?"

"I googled what a catamite is."

Wait. What. "Oh my God. Why?"

"Because your friend told me that's what you wanted to make me! Dude..." he darted in close and pulled down his sunglasses. He looked left and right. He took a deep breath. "Dude—"

I took a step back and closed the door in his face.

You know when you kind of just look at a situation and say, 'nope'?

Well, yeah.

Nope.

A rapid knock at my door. Of course.

"Dude!" His irritating voice was muffled through my front door, but, unfortunately, I could still hear him speaking. "Dude, why did your friend say you wanna have buttsex with me? That's weird, man! I'm not like... I'm not like a fag, you know?"

There it was.

"I need you to recognize that by slamming the door in your face I was giving you the opportunity to not say that part," I explained. "Ah, well. They were probably wondering why I don't like you. They probably thought I was being a jerk unnecessarily. Well, now they know."

They, meaning my friends. I whipped out my phone to shoot them a text.

Me: Blake the mistake dropped the f word. Now you see?

Their responses came in pretty quickly.

Kay: dude, ouch

Christi: what?? Fuck him man, this is the twenty-first century. People should not fucking be using that terminology anymore.

Ben: he said fuck?

Me: He said fag, Ben. Stop pretending like you're so straight that you don't pick up on LGBTQ+ issues.

Ben: fuck you man, I'm straight. And i get your gay shit ok? ... im just not gay. At all. Like ever you know?

Oh, Ben. Ben, Ben, Ben. Sweet, clueless Ben.

... Anyway.

Right. There was still knocking. Oh, and I needed to go to school.

Ben: not that i dont respect you being gay, i just am not. but i love you man, not in a gay way, but i totally can understand your issues and shit

Me: Ben, you're texting like someone who's panic-talking to get through an awkward conversation. But you can revise your texts, so I don't know what's wrong with you. Anyway, goodbye, Blake is knocking at my door.

Kay: You were just talking to him?

Kay: You mean you aren't walking with him rn? Why did u talk to him and now he's knocking on ur door? That's weird??

Kay: jake?,

I decided to put my phone away. "Blake, please leave, you're going to wake up my family. My cat doesn't like loud noises."

"Your cat is your family?"

"What? No? I have parents and a sister. You're my neighbor, don't you know this?"

I wasn't surprised that he didn't. Beckson was just that kind of inconsiderate person.

"Well sorry man, I kinda thought you were living on your own in a Batcave or something. I never see your family. Now can you open the door finally?" He sounded whiny again. Irritating.

"Yes, my family doesn't throw obnoxiously large cookouts once a month. That's true," I said. I admit it, I was a little salty. They were terrible neighbors, okay? Terrible. "Also, no. I want to go to school."

"What? Then come out of your house."

"But you're outside."

"...Okay, this whole 'I hate Blake' thing was really funny before I realized it was legit, but now it's kinda bothering me. And by bothering me, I mean it's lowkey hurting my feelings. Lowkey, though."

I sighed. He made me do that often. It was probably because the straights who wore joggers had such low IQs. "Blake, never say lowkey again please. Also, you know what lowkey hurts my feelings?"

He was quiet for a moment. It probably took a while for his four brain cells to power up.

"Uh, I'm not sure. My existence, or something?"

"No, Blake. The word fag hurts my feelings... Lowkey, though."

"Oh. Hey, open the door. We can talk about it on the walk."

Ugh. What was I thinking?

Blake and I talked on the walk, but I kept a three feet distance away from him. Enough to have a conversation, but also if we stopped talking we could pass as enemies.

"—which kinda fucked me up, ya know? It's not like I think being gay is a bad thing, because that's just stupid, but that's just what I associate it with. Every time one of my parents said gay, it was because I was doing something that wasn't meeting their standards. So I'm sorry, I am, but I also wanted you to know that it's not personal. I have gay friends! And it goes back to early childhood, so—"

He was also coming up with a million reasons why he was Not A Homophobe. Of course. That was so Blake Beckson of him.

I took a step away. There, now it was a whole four foot distance.

The old lady with the cookies was watering her garden. That meant we were close to the school. Good. "Hi, Blakey! Have fun at school you two! Thank God it's Friday!"

Oh, great, now the sweet old lady was brainwashed.

"Thanks, Nancy!" Blake answered with an overzealous wave.

I waved too, but charmingly. Subtly. Blake eyed my wave and I could tell he was judging me. His weird sparkly green eyes narrowed in on me.

He had this odd way of staring that made me feel like I couldn't look away. I hated it.

"You know you don't have to be so stoic all the time, right?" Beckson said. He turned those freaky green eyes on me and they locked on. "You tend to weird people out."

I turned to him and glared. "More insults? Was calling me a fag not enough for you?"

"Okay, I did not do that! When did I do that? That didn't happen. I said that I'm not a gay person. ...If it did happen, ya know, it wasn't serious or anything."

"Do I need to make Ben give you the n-word speech? He doesn't like to give it, but he will if he has to," I threatened.

"...Sorry." Blake shifted uncomfortably. "The n-word speech? Listen, man, I'm really sorry about saying that word and offending you and shit. Uh, the other word, not the n-word. I don't say that word."

He was fiddling with his fingers. I noticed that his nails were picked down to the skin and he had red spots where hangnails had been pulled off. He had a ring on his pinky finger. Huh. Wonder what that was about?

Ew, wait, no.

I looked away, because his hands were distracting. Oh look, we were at school. Thank. God. I didn't have to deal with any more of Blake's moronic insensitivity and blatant disregard of his own privilege.

And there was Kay! Thank God.

I made a beeline towards her and felt Blake's laser eyes on me the whole way over.

"I know what you're going to say and I do not care. I got your text at 6 freaking 40 AM, so I'm up-to-date." Those were the first words out of Kay's mouth. She barely paused from texting to glance up at me.

"I talk about things besides Blake," I said, not at all defensively. I did. I talked about school, and my family, and my cat.

"Okay, buddy," she said. "Sure."

"Anyway. School."

"Right, school. Let's go, we got homeroom," Kay said. "And then English III. You know, with that boy you like."

I blinked. Then I blinked again. Then I coughed, because it bought me some time. "Uh. Yeah."

"Knew it was fake."

"Oh, yeah. That guy! I just thought he was hot. Yeah, he's in that class." Was that sweat on my forehead? Fuck, I hated being a tank of a human. I needed to lose a few. Become one of those skinny boys.

But that would mean quitting my workout routine. Sad face. How about no.

"That's funny," Kay said. "You know who's in English III? Squad—" Me, her, Benny, and C, "—Kevin who plays trombone, Gavin the stoner, greasy Gabe, and Blake."

I frowned. "You got me. I think that playing trombone is so sexy."

"Wow, only Jake freaking Edwards can say a sentence like that without any emotion at all!" Ben's voice. Where was he?

Oh, right. I had to look down.

Ah, there he is!

"Hello, Ben."

"Hey, Jake."

Aw, look at him. He had a red hat that was the same shade of red as his shoes. That was so fancy. Ben always looked nice.

"Would you please stop looking at me like that? Creeps me out." Ben glared at me. "Makes me feel like you're undressing me with your eyes or something."

"Why do you guys only talk about how much you wanna fuck each other?" Kay asked, with an excessive eye roll. Oh wow, she had on a lot of eyeliner. It even ended in a fun little tip at the edges, that was cool. It looked hard to do.

"I don't want to fuck Ben," I explained. "I want to fuck someone else. You know. English III boy. Kevin."

Ugh. Kevin was so not the kind of person that people, like, wanted to fuck. At all. I definitely should have picked a better guy to have a fake crush on.

Why did I have a fake crush again? When did this happen?

Oh well. Now I had to roll with it.

My friends decided to give each other knowing looks and ignore me. We all walked into school together and, for once, I actually glanced around. Usually I was too preoccupied with Blake.

The school was ugly. Not because it was old or anything, but because it had white and orange tiles with red walls. And yellow lockers, with some rust around the edges. And a ton of posters about cyberbullying, which, really? Wasn't that term outdated?

I found my yellow locker and snatched my English book. We were reading One Hundred Years of Solitude, which pretty much sounded like my ideal life.

I stepped into the classroom and sought out my squad, as Kay put it. Christi and Ben were in the corner. We usually took the four seats in the back corner, because Ben liked to be the kid who made witty comments and pretended to slack off. He said the back was his zone.

We all just kind of followed Ben's lead.

I plopped down in the back row next to Christi. Kay was late, because even though she was 5 feet tall and wore pretty dresses exclusively, she liked to pretend she was a badass.

I was jerked out of my daydreaming by a bag dropping next to me. Except that wasn't right, because Kay was supposed to sit in front of Christi. I glanced over.

Oh no.

It was Blake.

Chapter Four

"Leave," I blurted.

He made an annoyed noise and that mouth of his pulled down at the corners. I hated that look, it was so pouty and I just wanted to hit him. "Dude."

And he always said dude. Why did he do that? Why did he do that?

Christi laughed. "Hey Blake." She smiled. Her smile had a thousand stars in it, it was so dazzling. It was the, Oh, Blake, stop it! smile that girls always gave him.

"Hey." He gave it back a thousand times better. His kind of bushy, but not too bushy, eyebrows even quirked up a little. His left cheek dimpled. His slightly crooked, but not too crooked, front tooth showed. The light, light splash of freckles on his nose rippled with his grin. His green eyes sparkled.

He was so unbelievable.

Literally. He was so fake. There was no way that was real. Black Beckson was a big show for the rest of the world. A privileged little asshole who pretended to be so sweet.

"Oh look who it is!" Ben looked positively delighted. "Blake! Good to see you!" I tried to glare a hole into the back of his skull, but it unfortunately didn't work.

I turned my attention to Blake. "Why are you stalking me?"

He seemed genuinely confused. "I just want to sit here. Why is that about you at all?"

"Yes, of course it is. Before today, you sat there." I pointed to his usual seat across the room, next to Kelly and Claire. They were only two of his excessively large group of friends. People tended to flock to Blake like he was a light and they were a ton of fat, ugly moths.

Blake's eyes did their weird light-up thing. It was some odd combination of his eyes widening and then some underlying glee that filled his usually neutral expression. "You noticed where I sit?"

"Yes. Do I win a metal?"

"Oh shut up. You don't have to be such a dick all the time." He plopped into the chair right when Dr. Clark and Kay walked into the room. Kay waved at us and sat down.

I glared at Blake as Dr. Clark turned on the classroom lights, causing everyone to groan. "I'm not a dick. You're a dick."

Blake stared me right in the eyes. He hesitated, then raised his pointer finger to his lips. "Shh."

He was the worst.

"Okay, as you all know, we're going to be starting our projects in class today," Dr. Clark said, pausing to blow her nose with a tissue.

Project?

I scootched closer to Ben, farther from Blake. Wait a minute. Oh no. Oh no.

"You have to move," I whispered to Blake. He gave me a ridiculous look.

"Why?"

Oh no. This can't happen to me. Not today.

What kind of evil cliché was this?

"I'm going to parter you up by location in the classroom," Dr. Clark droned on. "Then you can get in your groups and begin to discuss the aspect of the book you'll like to present on. The options will be on the board. Okay, I'll start. Kevin, Kate, and Gavin, you'll be working together. Alana—"

No.

My hand shot up. "Can I go to the bathroom?"

Dr. Clark's eyebrows raised. "Right now? Jake, you just had your morning break."

"I know, but I was a little late and I needed to grab my book instead," I blurted. Which wasn't actually a lie. Thanks, Blake, for not letting me leave my house.

"Okay. Well, we'll have to give you a partner before you go. Why don't you work with Blake?"

Oh, dammit!

"Uh, Blake and I don't really live close—"

"We'll make it work! Won't we, Jake?" Blake gave me a dazzling smile.

"I guess we'll have to," I grumbled. Then I walked off to go to the bathroom, tail between my legs.

The second class was out, I shoved Blake up against a locker.

"What the hell?" I snarled, grabbing at his shirt.

"Dude! I told you I'm not gay, stop pushing me up against the wall!" Blake cried. He looked actually kind of pissed, which was a new one for him.

"You are so annoying."

I dropped him and walked away. Of course, he trailed after me. Because apparently Blake was obsessed with me now.

"So do you do that often? Just brutally shove people into walls? Because you should probably go to therapy."

"Shut up."

"I'm just saying," he said, blinking up at me through the brown curls of hair on his forehead. "I'm really into psychology, and anyone who studies the psychodynamic model will tell you that you probably have some fucked up unconscious motivation for—"

"Yeah, it's my hatred for you and your homophobia," I muttered. Okay, I was still salty from the morning.

"Homophobia? C'mon, man, you don't really think that, right? I'm not."

I paused at my locker and silently prayed that he would go away. When that didn't work, I decided to shove my books into my locker and ignore his existence.

"I'm not a homophobe. Just because I said a bad word once doesn't make me a homophobe. I just slipped up for a second. I like gay people."

I turned around and stared at Blake Beckson. He was less than a head short-er than me, probably forty pounds of muscle smaller than me, and had a weird open innocence that made girls follow him around like puppies. He wore Nike brand shoes and mid-high socks and shorts that were a little too baggy.

He was such a straight boy.

"I'm not a homophobe, Jake," Blake insisted. I stared into his green eyes and had to stop myself from grinning when he fidgeted. He even began to blush a little, which looked even more stupid when he scowled. "I'm not. I talk to you and I talk to Christi, and she's pansexual. Oh and my friend Kelly, from English? She's bi. Also, my dad experimented with hot tub sex with a guy in college. So fuck you."

He finished his rant by looking away and crossing his arms.

"You're so..." I trailed off, looking for a word. "Theatric."

Blake squinted at me. "Are you trying to see if I'm going to make a theatre joke?"

I stared at him. Then stared some more. Then I decided that, considering I only got a couple hours of sleep last night and I had a statistics test in my third period, I didn't need to deal with this shit.

"Oh... is that Kay calling my name?" I said, with, admittedly, not a convincing amount of emotion. "Oh, no. A shame. Goodbye, Blake."

Out of all the times I've walked away from Blake Beckson, this one was the most relieving. I closed the door to my second period class and let out a breath. He actually managed to not follow me.

I sat through my European history course, trying not to nod off. It was difficult when the lecture was about the heretics of the 13th century in Italy. So lame.

A flash of movement by the door caught my attention. I glanced up, expecting it to be a teacher or something.

But, no. It was Blake.

He was looking through the glass of the door like an idiot. One hand was curled into a fist against the glass. His eyes darted about like he was trying to follow the movement of a fly, until they landed right on me.

His whole body stilled. A heartbeat passed, and then he was grinning wide and waving mockingly. I waiting until Mr. Shane's back was turned before flipping Blake off.

His grin widened and he made a vile motion with two fingers and his tongue. My nose wrinkled and he laughed.

I put my head on the desk.

A boring class and thirty minutes later, I found Blake lounging outside the classroom door. "Why are you standing here?" I demanded.

Blake glanced up from his phone. "We need to talk about our project."

"Thanks for that, by the way."

"What the hell did I do? Dr. Clark paired us together. Not my fault."

"You sat next to me!"

"Oh, so suddenly being friendly is a crime?"

"You aren't being friendly! You're being... manipulative! You knew she was going to give us a project!"

I glanced around once I noticed that my volume had gone up significantly. People were shooting us some pretty judgemental looks. Someone even turned to their friend and whispered, "Whoa, I didn't realize Jake had, like, emotion."

Blake scowled at me, which caught my attention. Huh. I always had a negative emotion associated with Beckson in my brain, but he never actually... acted negative.

"Everyone knew there was a project," Blake snapped. "She announced it seven times. Sorry for actually focusing on my school work instead of sports."

I focused on school work. I had to. If I got less than a C in a class, they kicked me off the team. "I don't just focus on track," I grumbled. "... It's not even outdoor track season yet."

Blake snorted. "You're such a jock."

"First I was what you called me this morning, now I'm a jock?" That also got me some incredulous glances from people around me. "You're Blake Beckson, the golden child of the junior class. So fuck you."

"Fuck you, I didn't call you any name! And I don't even know what you're talking about!"

"Oh please, you practically have a cult following. Your little clique is a group of the most popular people in the grade."

Blake rolled his eyes and tucked his phone in his pocket. "This conversation is stupid. I'm leaving. We're hanging out at my house tonight."

My stomach dropped. Blake Beckson's presence, for more than an hour? Oh shit. "You can't do this to me."

"Oh, shut up. I think you can survive a conversation with me."

No. No, I'm pretty sure I could not do that at all.

...Well, guess we'd find out.

Chapter Five

W alking up to Blake Beckson's porch was a force. It felt weird to be willingly subjecting myself to torture. Willingly entering the cave of the monster. Willingly dragging myself into the depths of hell.

"Will you move?" Blake snapped. He was standing directly behind me, with his cool kid shades on.

"I don't know if I can do it." I stared at the door looming in front of me. It was white, had a thin, rectangular window next to it, the same height as the door.

There was a little knocker in the middle of the door, shaped like an anchor. This state was landlocked. ...Creepy.

"Fuck you." Blake pushed past me and entered his home. There was a distant squeal of delight. It sounded motherly. I had a vague memory of his mom from a cookout over the summer, she seemed like a lot to deal with.

If I left now, I could get to my door in 4 seconds at a sprint.

"Come on, Jake!" Blake yelled from inside. Dammit. Too late now, his mother knew I was here.

I sighed. "...Coming."

I was greeted with a similar delighted squeal, and I was practically assaulted with a tray of cookies. What was with people and cookies? What was with the Beckson family and being irritating?

"Oh, hi Jake Edwards!" Ms. Beckson said. She sort of looked like an almost-middle-aged white women from any of the Grimm's fairy tales. She was plump, wore an apron, and was bearing cookies.

I glanced at the oven to make sure I wouldn't fit inside.

"Hi, Ms. Beckson. It smells good in here." See, I could be polite. The kitchen did, in fact, smell like cookies.

"Oh, have a cookie, you must be so hungry! I bet you must eat a lot to have such big muscles! And you're so tall too! I always told Henrietta that she had such a handsome son!"

When did she talk to my mom? Why was it that I could literally see the exclamation marks at the ends of her sentences? Also was she into me?

"Oh, no thank you. I don't want to spoil dinner later," I said, giving the tray of cookies a polite smile.

"Oh, please!" she scoffed. "Just one! I won't tell your mom." She wiggled her eyebrows as if there were some incredible secret between us. As if originally she planned on telling my mother that I ate a cookie before dinner. Her green eyes widened.

Okay, well there was only one way out of this situation. "Ah. Well as long as you don't tell." I took a cookie and flashed her a smile.

Blake rolled his eyes.

"Thanks, Ma. We gotta get to work now though," he grumbled.

"Aw, am I embarrassing you in front of the sweet neighbor boy?" she asked, batting her eyelashes.

She turned to me and dropped me a wink. ... Definitely could be into me. That was horrifying.

Blake's face flushed red. "You weren't. Now you kind of are."

"Aw, oops. You run along, boys." She fixed a stern look on Blake. "I don't wanna hear that door close, Mister."

I didn't think it was possible for Blake's face to get any redder. "Why, Ma?"

"Oh, you know." She looked at me and Blake covered his face with his hands. She winked. "Drugs and things, that's all. Run along, boys."

Blake groaned. "Come on, Jake."

He walked away and I grinned at Ms. Beckson. "Thanks for the cookies, ma'am."

"Oh, anytime, sweetheart!"

"Come on, Jake!"

With a last smile, I followed Blake to his room. The second his door shut, I gasped and massaged my face. "I'm exhausted. That was a lot of smiling."

Blake blinked at me. "You smiled once."

"Three times. It was hard."

"I hate you."

I kept rubbing my face and glared at him. "I hate you substantially more. Apparently you've convinced your mother that I'm a drug dealer."

Blake stared at me a beat too long. "Yeaaah. That's what she meant. Totally. Okay. Um, let's get to work."

I huffed and plopped down onto him swirly chair. Blake Beckson's bedroom was a weird room. I had been expecting a mess akin to your common town dump, with maybe one conveniently located shelf filled with trophies of his great athletic accomplishments, but there was no such thing.

There was a clean brown rug and an already-made bed (that was weird, Blake was weird, also he was Satan, who makes their bed?). The messiest part of his room was his bookshelf, which had a bunch of books stacked around and on top of it. The only other part of his room that showed signs of life was his desk. It had some books and opened snacks, including a half-eaten Hostess Ding Dong and a banana.

He also had a little sticky note on his computer which said, "Don't forget to call Gram and tell her good luck!" What kind of monster needed a note to call his grandma?

Blake Beckson was a savage.

"Uh, Jake, you gonna stop looking around my room like a weirdo? C'mon dude I wanna actually do some work."

"Sorry, I just expected it to be a lot different," I admitted with a shrug.

Blake gave me a bland look. "What? No hellfire? No corpses or little children I captured and forced to do my bidding? No jars of human bits floating in formaldehyde?"

"...The depth of detail you can go into alarms me."

"Yeah, okay, you really sound alarmed," he scoffed. "Besides, what's so weird about my room? It's just a room."

I stared into his beady little green eyes. "Well. I figured it would be more narcissistic." He gave me a blank stare. "You know. Like, trophies. And mirrors. And pictures of you and your million friends doing really fun things."

That got a flash of emotion. Emotion? Blake Beckson? Amazing. "Wow. I really think I might punch you in the face if you talk one more time."

Ah, ever the brute. "I'm not surprised that you're into unnecessary violence."

"Me?!" he sputtered. "You tossed me against a locker!"

Hmm. I did do that. "It was for a good reason. I did nothing wrong. You never hear people complain when the hero of a movie slays the villain."

Blake wiped a hand down the side of his face, further showcasing his lack of patience or general positive qualities. "Can we please just work on this project?"

"I don't even know what it's about."

"Shocking."

Now he was going to be sarcastic with me? Rude. "The only reason I don't know is because you distracted me all class by existing in my personal bubble."

"I sat in the desk next to you, only because that stupid little trombonist Kevin took my seat!"

"I want to fuck him, so shut up!" Then I blinked and remembered I needed to really get my shit together. "Wait, no—"

"Kevin? You want to fuck trombonist Kevin? What the hell? First of all, he plays trombone. Second of all, he has a man bun. Third of all, he wears Crocs!" Blake flopped himself down onto his bed and groaned.

Of course Benson was into judging people based off of their looks rather than their personality traits. He was like that.

"He happens to be a nice guy. But if you let me finish, I actually don't want to fuck him." Why was I telling him this again? Mouth, stop. "I lied to my friends so they'd stop bothering me about boys."

About you.

I didn't say that part.

My life was ass.

Blake Benson gave me a heavy stare and a slow blink. "I don't actually care. At all."

He was infuriatingly rude. "You are so annoying."

"Usually I'd care," he continued. "I'm into helping people solve their personal problems." Wow, what a saint. "But you're mean to me. So I don't care about your problems at all."

"Okay, good. I don't care about your problems. At all."

"Good."

"Good."

He glared at me and I stared blankly back. Eventually, something shifted in his electric green eyes. "But why the hell are you lying to your friends? Don't you realize that's wrong?"

"Not your business."

Benson groaned and flopped back onto his bed. "Fine. We pick an overarching thematic topic shown in One Hundred Years of Solitude and then we analyze it."

That sounded like a load of boring. Also, confusing. "How do we analyze it?"

"You know..." He wrinkled his little nose and made a funny face. It was almost a frown, except his pink lips were pouty. "We figure out the message he's trying to send, cite examples of it in the book, find connecting examples of symbolism, stuff like that."

"Ah. Would you like to do that part? I can do something else, just tell me what part I should do."

Please, give me something better. Please.

Instead, he gave me a long look of one who'd lost all hope. "You're going to be an awful partner, I can already tell."

He was awful. "What do you mean? I understand that you're big on being judgmental, but seriously. This is ridiculous."

"Jake, the analyzing and writing is the entire project. You can't just do something else. We need to work together," Blake said. His tone was low and slow, like he was talking to a very stupid person. Great. Now I had 'condescending' to add to my list of Beckson's character flaws.

"I can't think of anything worse than this moment right here, with you," I informed him.

Blake blinked and I got caught up in those green eyes of his. They were just so disgusting that they took my breath away. It was like God made him right after he made the Everglades and he had some extra swamp water left over.

"You're an asshole," Blake said.

"You're a monster."

"Fine, whatever," Blake said. "I get that you hate me, but we need to start to get along. I have the perfect plan. We're going to play a game together."

...This was going to be horrible.

Chapter Six

"Are you ready for our game?" Blake Beckson asked me. His usually pouty mouth was set in a hard line. This nasty green eyes were focused in on me. I had his entire attention, unfortunately.

"Ah. No."

I'd read enough gay fiction to know where games lead to. I did not want to go there with Blake.

His disgustingly determined look faltered just a little bit at my response. Deep down, I was satisfied to see his weakness. "Wait, really?" he whined.

"Really," I confirmed. "I refuse to play a game with you."

"But Twenty Questions is pretty—"

"I don't care. I refuse."

We sat in awkward silence, staring at each other. Eventually, he shrugged and sighed. "Well, alright then."

So weak-willed.

"Let's finish this project already," I said. Blake was such an unhelpful partner, always trying to get us off topic.

He had the audacity to facepalm. "I just had to spend ten minutes explaining the project to you, because you can't pay attention in class for shit. All you ever do is talk to that little boyfriend of yours."

Boyfriend?

I was genuinely confused. I knew Blake didn't care about anyone but himself, but was he really so detached from reality that he thought I was in a relationship?

"...Kevin? The trombonist?"

"No! You don't even like Kevin I thought!"

"I don't."

"Then what the fuck, man?"

Ugh, his voice was so annoying. Once when I was a kid, I visited a farm. One of the farmhands accidentally fell and landed on a pig. Blake's voice sounded alarmingly similar to the sound that the pig made after being fallen on.

When Blake realized I was too annoyed by his general characteristics to answer, he rolled his eyes and continued insensitively dominating the conversation. "Ben, obviously."

Before I realized what I was doing, I was tipping my head back and laughing. In fact, I cackled so hard and for so long that my stomach actually started to hurt.

Ben? My boyfriend?! Blake was tapped.

"Are you laughing?" Blake asked, an oddly alarmed look on his face.

"Are you stupid?"

"Wow, thanks." Blake shook his head, but he still had a kind of dazed and flushed expression on. I wasn't convinced that he wasn't stupid. "Um, I've never heard you laugh before."

"Maybe you're just not funny," I considered, which made the flush on Blake's face completely disappear. Instead, it was replaced by anger.

"Okay, fine, it's time to work on our project so I don't have to talk to you anymore," he said grumpily.

For the first time ever, I could actually agree with Blake on something.

He made me pick a theme out of a whole list and then we searched through the book for related quotes. I was enjoying the peace and quiet of Blake Beckson's silence, until he began talking twenty minutes into our searching.

"It's fine if Ben's your boyfriend," Blake said randomly. I stifled my chuckles. "I can tell that you're into each other, even though he's obviously in the closet."

"Blake, you're so wrong. So, so wrong," I said, amused. "Ben would probably kill you if he heard you say something like that about him. Even though he's definitely gay, he hates it when people assume that. Plus I would never like Ben."

"Why?" Blake said, an odd look on his face. "What kind of guys do you like?"

Why Blake Beckson cared what kind of guy I liked was absolutely beyond me, but I liked this topic of conversation. Since Blake was a homophobe, it was either numbing his hatred for gay people or making him uncomfortable.

Win win either way.

I hummed, truly thinking about it. "Well, I generally like guys who are short and sort of athletic, but not super muscular like I am. And they have to be good at school, because it's kind of hot when people are smart. I like curly brown hair and green eyes and men who care about other people."

Blake Beckson was giving me an absolutely flabbergasted expression.

"Of course," I added sadly, "There's nobody out there like that really."

Blake blinked.

"Why are you staring at me like that?" I snapped. "You're so weird."

"I think you're really stupid," Blake said. He glared at me and his green eyes were doing that piercing thing again. "There's people out there like that. Closer than you'd expect."

I leaned forward and studied him, trying to get a good read. But nope, all I saw was a load of annoying Blake. "Are you trying to be motivating? To make up for calling me a fag?"

"I didn't do that!" Blake threw his hands in the air and shot me the most exasperated look ever. "And you're ridiculous! I'm like that. You just described me, word for word, and yet you totally hate me! Clearly you aren't really sure what your type actually is."

I scoffed. "I did not describe you. You're not sho...well, you aren't athletic ...huh. I guess the hair and eye color was right too." This was very alarming and perplexing. But then I remembered the one very important detail and calmed down. "You don't care about other people."

Because yes, physically, Blake was exactly what I would want in another man. But there was so much more to an attractive person than their looks. And Blake didn't have a lot going for him on the morality side of things.

"How can you say that?" Blake whined. "You barely know me."

"I know enough," I scoffed. "Don't forget, I was your neighbor for years. I know the real you that you hide from other people."

The evil part.

Blake shook his head in wonder. "I have absolutely no fucking clue what you're talking about. Actually, that goes without saying for everything that comes out of your mouth."

Blake just didn't realize that I knew what I did. Because so many years ago, I witnessed Blake show his true colors. And he could pretend to be as kind as he wanted, and everyone in school could love him, and he could walk around looking adorable, but I wouldn't ever forget what he did that one summer...

Chapter Seven

Blake and I used to be close friends, back when he first moved into the neighborhood. I really liked his family and I really liked him, so for a while we were two peas in a pod.

That lasted maybe a month.

It was the same summer that I realized I was gay. I was about nine years old, and I had been hanging out at Blake's house. Blake had a pool that was a ton of fun, and we were both swimming in the same direction real fast to make the water move in one direction.

In our efforts to turn around and swim against the whirlpool, I collided against Blake and he'd held me for a second too long. We were both laughing and I'd gotten an up-close of those beautiful green eyes — at least, I thought they were beautiful at the time.

I realized I was gay then, so I did a lot of research on the subject. I kept my distance from Blake the whole next week as I was discovering more about myself and what I wanted in a romantic partner. Thanks to the internet, I realized that I was normal and there were others like me.

I wasn't too worried about the whole gay thing. I was going to tell Blake and resume life as normal. So that weekend, when the Beckson family had a neighborhood cookout, I planned to tell Blake.

However, something happened that changed everything.

I snapped out of my day dream with Blake waving and snapping in my face. "Hello? Earth to probably the meanest person I've ever met in my whole life? Can we please focus on the project?"

"Sorry, I was thinking about how much of a horrible person you are," I admitted honestly. Blake facepalmed.

I looked through my book until I'd found all the quotes I could. Blake and I wrote them all down on one piece of paper and at that point it had been over an hour. It was a small miracle that Blake and I had actually managed to work together to get something done.

"So next, all we have to do is come up with a thesis based on our topic that you picked and use these quotes to support it," Blake explained. I really hated how condescending he was, acting like I needed constant explanation.

Considering I actually was really lost and confused on the project, though, I didn't mention it.

"Can we do that part later?" I asked. "I've had enough of you for one day."

Blake scowled and shook his head. His brown and curly hair went flying from side to side when he did that. "No, we're not done yet. I want to do well on this, so we can't just wait until last minute to do this stupid project."

I sighed and settled my head in my hands. "I take it back, men who do good in school aren't my type."

"Please stop being a stereotypical athlete for one second?" Blake asked, sounding like he was begging. "You're actually so annoying. Let's just do schoolwork, it isn't the worst thing."

I settled down on his bed and accepted my fate. Blake the snake was keeping my trapped in his home to never leave, torturing me with school.

After a few more minutes of silent working, Blake plopped his feet in my lap and rested his back against the wall. I stared at his feet like they'd personally offended me, which they had, but Blake didn't actually care.

And I was scared to touch him more than I had to, so his feet remained on my lap.

My rule was definitely being broken. If anyone walked in, they would totally think that we were friends. Maybe even more than friends. Horrifically, his mom opened the door right as I was thinking about it happening.

"Blake!" she said, a scowl on her face. She rested her hands on her hips. "What did I say about keeping this door open? You're lucky I didn't catch you two doing anything inappropriate, or you would be in so much trouble."

Why was she so convinced that I was a drug dealer?

"Sorry about scolding my son in front of you, Jake honey," she added and batted her lashes at me, because she was totally into me.

Once she left, I realized I had a slightly different problem. My hands were holding a piece of paper meant to 'brainstorm thesis ideas,' which I wasn't doing, which thankfully covered my crotch.

However, having a guy's body parts so close to my crotch was not having the type of effect I needed when I was around Blake the snake.

But then he yawned, lifting his arms up and allowing the bottom of his shirt to ride up his stomach. This exposed a sliver of tan and firm skin, which didn't help my problem. Almost like he knew what he was doing, Blake dragged his shirt up with one hand and scratched his stomach, exposing even more skin.

This was not good.

I tossed the paper in his face and stood up. "You're not the boss of me." I grabbed my bag and walked out of the room. "I'm leaving."

I managed to make it all the way out of the house before he appeared behind me, looking pissed.

"You can't just leave for no reason!" Blake huffed. He waved the book in my face. "This is important."

If I stuck around any longer, he was going to see the massive boner that he caused.

"I have to be going for dinner," I said. "We'll work on it tomorrow."

I walked away and Blake apparently decided it wasn't worth it, because he yelled an expletive and slammed his house door when he went back inside.

That night, I dreamt of Blake. My subconscious betrayed me by feeding me images of Blake naked and underneath me. His green eyes were electric and his face was flushed.

I woke up the next day absolutely cursing his name. Even when he wasn't around, Blake was causing me trouble.

Chapter Eight

My walk to school was awkward. All I could really focus on was my previous dream. Suddenly my typical routine of walking ten feet behind Blake was not a good one, because I'd never realized how tightly his ugly joggers hugged his ass before.

He waved to Nancy and a couple other neighbors, because he had to keep up his kind act. I knew better.

But still, when he waved his bicep flexed in a really distracting way.

I was losing my mind if I thought that Blake Beckson, bane of everyone's existence, was handsome.

Thankfully he was still mad at me for leaving yesterday, so he didn't harass me like he had been for the previous couple days. I approached Ben without any interruption.

"Okay, so here's my plan," Ben said instead of saying hi. He clapped his hands together and gave me an all-business look. "You're obviously too shy to say anything to him, so I say we start leaving notes in his locker. Pretty soon he'll be in love and you'll be able to admit that you're the man behind the letters."

"That sounds like a bad love story," I critiqued. "Also, who is this for? Blake?"

Ben blinked. "Uh. No. It's for Kevin the trombonist."

Ah. Right. Awkward.

"I'll talk to Kevin," I promised. "We don't have to do this whole crazy plan, I'll just come up with a way to woo him today."

Which was how, a few hours later, I ended up talking to Kevin the trombonist after English. I could literally feel the weight of Ben's excited look on my back. Oh, and Blake's glare.

He was seriously still mad about the night before? The guy needed a hobby.

Kevin stumbled and dropped his book when he saw me, and I grabbed it before it could even hit the ground. A blush came over his entire face. "J-jake? Um, hi there. I mean, thank you. For catching my book."

I handed it back to him and he blushed even further. "It wasn't a problem. Kevin, I need to speak with you about something important."

He nibbled on his chapped bottom lip and leaned in further. "Oh. Okay, about what?"

He really was not handsome. And he was wearing crocs, Blake was right.

"I... I have realized recently that I have feelings for you," I lied through my teeth, feeling pretty bad for Kevin. But I could hear Ben doing a not-so-quiet victory dance in the corner behind me.

Kevin's eyes widened and he even gasped. His blush got even worse. "You do?" His eyelashes fluttered as he blinked in amazement. "But you're like... you're like the hottest gay guy in school."

There was only one other gay guy in our school besides the two of us. His nickname was literally greasy Gabe.

"No," I protested, likely with not a lot of passion. "You are."

Kevin blushed and stuttered even more. "W-want to go on a date sometime?"

I really didn't. "Yes."

He smiled and said something awkward and waved and tripped before making it all the way to the classroom door. Then he blushed even more, collected himself, and walked out like a normal human being.

"Young love!" Ben burst out, giving me a solid round of applause. Kay and Christi looked baffled and Blake still looked pissed, not that it mattered. "I'm such a great wingman!"

Right, my acting wasn't over yet. I forced a smile. "Thanks, Ben. I've been working up the nerve to do that all year."

Ben hugged me and wiped away fake tears. "No problem, big guy. Happy to help. And you're already a pro! I see that you didn't get his number so that you got the chance to talk to him again."

Uh. Fuck. Now I had to talk to him again.

"You caught me."

—//—

After lunch, I decided it was time to approach Kevin the trombonist and fake man of my dreams once again. However, I found him pressed up against a locker by Blake the snake.

Blake had his arms on either side of Kevin and the poor kid's trombone was on the ground a few feet to the right. "He doesn't actually like you," Blake was saying. "He told me that his friends were bugging him about boys so he picked you to get them off his back."

Kevin set his jaw and glared, though he was clearly terrified. "He said he likes me!"

Blake made a frustrated noise and stepped away. "Whatever, man! I'm just trying to tell you the truth. Stay away from Jake."

I probably could have swooped in and told Kevin that Blake was a lying liar, but instead I turned on my heel and walked away. It was better that Kevin knew the truth so that his feelings weren't hurt.

What had Blake's goal been? Was he trying to ruin my life?

For once, I doubted it. It seemed like he was doing it more for Kevin's benefit than mine. For some reason, I didn't actually feel overwhelming hatred for Blake when I thought of it that way.

—//—

On the walk back, Blake was way more chatty than he had been for the walk up.

"Alright, we're finishing our project today," he decided, because apparently Blake was the king of everything. "And you aren't running away all scared this time."

"Why is your goal to ruin my life?" I asked, figuring I could just try to get answers out of him.

"...What are you talking about?"

I sighed and shook my head, disappointed that he even bothered to pretend. "I saw you talking to Kevin today. You told him the truth."

To my shock, Blake actually blushed. "You saw that?"

"Yes! What if I actually liked him?" I asked. It was kind of a long shot because as nice as Kevin was, he really wasn't my type. But still, it was the principle of the thing. "You could have ruined a really nice relationship."

"You shouldn't like him," Blake huffed. He even crossed his arms. "He's ugly and he's whiney and he wears crocs and plays the trombone."

"He's not whiney!"

"Well, he isn't your type judging by what you described last night!" Blake said. "You described someone like me; and it's insulting if you think I'm anything like that loser."

He was being kind of weird. Blake was usually the bane of my existence, but he wasn't really pissing me off.

That's why, when we finally settled into his bedroom, I was utterly shocked when Blake asked me out on a date.

Chapter Nine

"Would you want to go on a date with me?" Blake the evil snake asked me, green eyes wide and curious.

It took me approximately two seconds to come up with my answer. "Um, no. I hate you."

Blake threw his hands in the air. "No you don't! I'm your type and you got a boner yesterday when you were around me. You're overcompensating. And guess what? It's your lucky day, because I'm bisexual."

"No you're not."

"This is the most blatant example of bisexuality erasure that I've ever seen," he said, exasperated, and the words bisexuality erasire coming out of homophobic Blake's mouth made no sense.

"You're a homophobe," I accused. "I know you're a homophobe."

"Ask my mom!" Blake said. He stood up, tense and uncomfortable, and yelled, "MOM! Aren't I bisexual?!"

Distantly, his mom answered, "Yeah, sweetheart!"

Okay, he easily could have given his mother money to say something like that. I knew that Blake Beckson was a homophobe.

"See?" Blake's green eyes were trained on me. "I'm bisexual. And I'm not a homophobe. And I broke up with my girlfriend the second I found out we were working on this project together."

"Why?" I was utterly baffled. He seemed completely honest. Of course, Blake was a deceptive person, but still...

"Because, I want to..." Blake sighed. "I've always liked you a little bit, Jake. That's why I tried to talk to you all those times on the way to school. Remember back when we were friends? I liked you back then."

He was definitely fucking with me.

"I hate you Blake, we're not compatible."

"Why do you hate me so much? I just don't get it! There's no reason that I can think of."

Looks like I'd have to explain myself. "It was back when we were nine. The very week your family threw a big cookout, I realized I was gay." I didn't mention how I found out. "The same day I was going to tell you, I overheard you talking to some kid at the cookout. You were mad at him and called him a stupid homo," I recalled. "You pushed him to the ground and he started crying."

"That's why you hate me?" He stood up off the bed and faced me. He looked kind of pretty with his hair a mess and his face flushed in anger. "From something that stupid that happened nine years ago?"

"Yes!"

"That's insane!"

"...Too bad, I hold grudges."

Blake was looking at me with his jaw dropped. He shook his head. "That little snot's name was Drew and he totally had a crush on you. When he told me I acted like a dick."

"Yes. You're an asshole."

"I was jealous, you dumbass."

Wow, he was really putting it all out there.

"That's convenient to your 'oh I'm bi now' story," I scoffed.

Blake groaned and over-dramatically dropped face-first onto his bed. "Jake," he mumbled into his pillow. "I'm into guys and I think you're kind of okay."

I was really torn. On one hand, he was kind of my type. On the other...well I hate him for being a homophobe, but... if he actually wasn't...

"Are you fucking with me?" I asked honestly. "Because when Ben told you I wanted to do gay things with you, which wasn't true by the way, you said 'I'm not a fag.'"

He lifted his head from the pillow and I took in his blush and his shy look. "No," he admitted. I actually believed him. I actually didn't think that Blake was being a snake. "I'm not fucking with you. I only said that because nobody knows the truth about me and I was scared. ...I still am, to be honest."

Well, that was really all I needed. "Okay, I'll go on a date with you, not Kevin. Because I guess if you're not actually Satan incarnate, I need to figure out who you are."

Blake the not snake gave me a surprisingly bright smile. It seemed to light up the room. "Really?"

"Really. I guess."

—//—

The next day at school, I had the impossible task of telling Kevin that I wasn't actually interested in going on a date with him anymore.

"I'm not interested in going on a date with you anymore," I informed him tactfully.

Kevin nodded. "I-it's okay. Blake told me the truth."

"Yeah, sorry."

"It's okay."

Well that was easy.

With that awkward task over, I had some explaining to do. I sat down at my lunch table and met my friend's eyes. "You guys aren't going to believe it," I began.

They all asked me what was up.

"Don't freak out, but I'm going on a date tomorrow... with Blake Beckson," I said, truly expecting them to freak out.

Kay just shook her head. "Thank God the overcompensation is over."

"I knew you wanted to make him your catamite!" Ben exclaimed, way too loudly in the lunchroom.

Thankfully people were already used to him. Nobody looked over.

Christi was the nice one. "I'm happy for you, Jake. I know you've been crushing on him for a long time, so I hope the date goes well."

Everyone seemed to think that I was in love with him, except for me. I mean sure, when I truly got a glance of his green eyes, they gave me stomach flutters. And fine, there was no doubting that he was obviously very handsome and charming. But still—that was just admiring!

On the way home from school, I walked side-by-side with the guy I once hated and now was confused about.

"I hope this date goes poorly," I admitted. "It would be really tragic if I never got to call you Blake the snake ever again."

Blake rolled his eyes and let out a little laugh, which was new. He had a nice laugh, for a sicko. "You're way too blunt, do you know that?"

I shrugged. "I just tell the truth."

"Let's go on our date tomorrow," Blake suggested. "And if it goes well, we can go on another date."

I looked into green eyes that I'd once considered swamp water. Now I thought they more closely resembled emeralds.

Not that I liked emeralds, either.

"I really hope I don't regret this, Blake the snake."

Chapter Ten

Blake must have been some kind of evil mind-reading wizard. That was the only logical explanation for why he knew what my favorite activity was.

Besides track, my favorite thing to do was to go-cart. I barely ever got to do it, as it was a special occasion type of activity, but it was so much fun.

Slamming into other people relentlessly and then eventually beating them in a competition? That was my shit.

"I don't trust you," I said.

Blake raised his eyebrows. "Whoa, wait until the second date before you sweet talk me like that."

"How did you know?"

"Dude, you're getting all weird and cryptic again. How did I know what?" he asked.

I watched a bunch of people of all ages flying around the track in their cars. I was smiling before I could help myself. It just looked like so much fun.

"That I like go-cart racing," I said, hearing my voice drop to a whisper. It was kind of like I was reluctant to admit defeat.

Good thing Blake was obnoxious, though. He leaned in, tapped his ear, and went, "Huh?! Dude, what did you say?"

I gritted my teeth. "Mediocre date idea, snake."

"Ooh we've shortened Blake the snake to just snake now?" He gave me that toothy, happy smile and nudged me. "I'm starting to think you're sweet on me."

I used to think that smile was fake. Now I thought it was cute. There was only one reasonable explanation.

Blake had poisoned me.

"Blake, did you poison me?" I asked. "That's the only logical explanation for why I think you have a nice smile now."

To my complete and utter shock, Blake actually stopped in his tracks and stared at me, eyes wide and a blush on his cheeks. He looked so un-Blake-like in that moment. Not one ounce of confidence in him.

"...You like my smile?"

I should not have admitted that. But I'd come too far to turn back, so I nodded. "Wasn't it just yesterday that you said you're my type? You were confident then."

"Yeah, but, I don't know." He scowled. "That's the nicest thing you've ever said to me."

"Oh. I take it back then."

"You can't, no takesies-backsies," Blake yelped desperately. "You complimented me! Ha, that is so unnatural."

Definitely poison. This was not a likable boy.

I glanced at him and really observed. He was wearing a t-shirt with a cartoon skateboarder on it, even though I'd never seen him skateboard. More khaki joggers, except this time they were pulled up on his calfs a little to expose his tall socks that were covered in little pizzas. And he was wearing Vans.

I hated his fashion. I should've hated him.

But for whatever psychotic reason, I didn't.

"Fine, I guess I did compliment you," I admitted reluctantly. "Now that I know you're a scared and closeted bisexual it's hard to tote you as a homophobe."

Blake grabbed my arm and leaned in close. "Shhhh!" He said obnoxiously. His eyes darted frantically to the guy who was overlooking the go-carting course. "People don't, like, know that, dude."

The guy looked our way and Blake ripped his hand away from my arm.

"Aren't you on a date with a guy right now?" I grumbled. "Not that I care if it isn't a date. But I thought it was."

"It is!"

"Then why is it somewhere so public? If you were so worried about what people would think, why didn't you plan to take me somewhere were we were alone?"

Blake's eyes narrowed. "Are you coming onto me? Trying to get me alone? C'mon man, I don't put out that fast."

He was ridiculous. Still, I could feel my face getting hot at the idea of...no. I couldn't even go there. This was Blake.

"No," I sputtered. "I was not. I was noting a flaw in your logic."

He put his hands on his hips. I learned then that green eyes could really pack a hell of a bitchy look. "Only you could come onto someone and make it seem like you're actually being rude."

I sputtered some more. "I'm not trying to...offend your virtue."

Blake froze. Then he made a weird choking noise, then he burst into laughter. I stared as he nearly doubled over. His laughing fit faded to giggles, and when he managed to stand straight once again I noticed tears in his eyes. "Dude. I was fucking with you. Please stop talking about my virtue."

I'd never been on a date before, but I'd seen enough movies to know that this was not how they were supposed to go. I was not supposed to be fucked with on a date. This was a bad idea.

"I'm leaving," I decided.

"No!" Blake yelped. He reached out grabbed my arm and I made the mistake of looking back at him.

His eyes were wide with worry and his kissable mouth was partially open with surprise. Jeez, who decided to make someone who was so stupid, also so attractive? The sun was turning his hair to gold at the ends, where it was also curling and frizzing.

"Hey, don't leave." Blake's voice was a tad bit frantic. "Gosh, you're uptight. Sorry! Didn't mean to piss you off. I was only kidding, I know you'd never come onto me. Um. You're not going to leave, right?"

I wiggled the arm that he was holding in a vice grip. "It doesn't seem like I can."

He let me go.

He was looking at me with this nervous expression and he started absent-mindedly nibbling on a hang nail. I felt a little bad for making him feel so uncertain.

I cleared my throat awkwardly. "Um. Sorry. I don't like being teased."

"You don't like anything, man."

I glared.

"Sorry! Sorry. Jk. I mean, I'm just kidding. Sorry, you're making me nervous. Stop looking at me like that." His laughter was awkward and goat-like, which was not charming whatsoever. However, I'd built Blake Beckson up over the years into being this straight, macho asshole that I'd clearly forgotten how awkward and nervous he was.

I kind of liked nervous and awkward Blake.

I relented. "Fine, I'll stop glaring. I'm not even mad anyway. Let's go have fun." I held out my hand as a peacemaker. Then I remembered that Blake was in the closet and awkwardly pulled it back.

Blake set his shoulders and took a deep breath. "No, it's okay." He grabbed my hand and laced our fingers together. When he looked back up at me, a little bit of his confidence had come back. "Who cares who sees, right? I'm allowed to hold a guy's hand. Screw it."

I smiled and squeezed his hand. It fit perfectly in mine. As much as I hated to admit it, it felt kind of okay. "Screw it."

Chapter Eleven

I ended up kicking Blake's ass in go-carting. It was so much of a disaster that I ended up rear-ending his go-cart and causing the tire to pop.

While Blake was given another car and most likely prayed that we didn't have to pay for damages, I did laps around the six year olds like there was no tomorrow.

One of the six year olds even cried. What a fucking sore loser.

I was awesome at go-carting.

After I'd won my fifth round, I met Blake outside of the track. He was wearing his sunglasses and leaning up against the fence.

"I think I'm going to have to get insurance involved," he told me the second he showed up. "That was a hell of a rear end... you nearly totaled my vehicle. Cops are gonna show up any minute."

I snorted and grabbed his sunglasses off of his face. "Alright, fuck off. What are they going to do?"

"Nothing. I guess it wasn't included in the waiver we signed, so they can't hold us to anything," Blake shrugged. "They said they'd never seen anything like it before."

I grinned. "I'm exceptional."

Blake snorted. "Dude, you're psycho. I don't think I've ever met anyone as competitive as you are."

"Why would I try to lose?"

Blake pointed over to where a six year old was sobbing into her parent's shoulder.

I shrugged. "I don't see your point."

"Oh my God," Blake laughed. I found myself yet again distracted by him. The longer we were on this date the more appealing he seemed.

He held his hand out and smiled. I didn't even hesitate to take it.

"Let's go grab some food or something. I seriously hadn't expected you to try to kill me on our date, but looking back I should've thought of it," Blake said with a grin. Was he teasing again?

"I hate you," I said, "but not enough to kill you."

I figured he'd appreciate the statement. Instead he snorted and shook his head.

"Thanks," Blake sighed, a small grin on his face. "You're so sweet."

I was making him smile an awful lot. Annoying.

Then Blake did an awful thing: he rested his head on my shoulder as we walked. He had his arms wrapped around mine like a cobra.

"Are you showing me affection?" I grumbled. "Ew. That's disgusting, please let me go."

Blake glared at me. "We're on a date, dude. You let me hold your hand first!"

"You were only doing that to make me feel better," I accused, wishing I could shake Blake off. He was doing weird things to my emotions, which was confusing everything.

I didn't like Blake. I was giving him a chance as an apology for our previous misunderstanding. And for constantly keeping a ten foot distance between us. And for calling him Blake the snake. And Blake the mistake. And for talking about him badly behind his back for almost a decade. And for saying I had the flu every time my family was invited to one of his family's cookouts. And for—

"That's not true!" Blake sputtered. "I was awkward about it at first because I'm still in the closet, but there's nobody here that we know. I know 'cause I already looked around a bunch. And even if there was, maybe I should stop being in the closet. You're out and nobody makes fun of you for it."

Because I was, quite simply, an intimidating person. People made fun of Kevin and Greasy all the time.

If they made fun of me, I would give them a free ticket to the hospital. Everyone knew that.

"You're thinking of coming out?" I asked, wisely deciding not to share my malicious internal monologue.

He kicked a rock and unfurled himself from my arm. "I don't know, maybe. I'm bi and I've never liked a guy, so I kind of thought there was no point until now."

Relieving.

"Ah," I said. "Then don't; there's no point."

He glared at me.

I blinked.

"What?" I asked. "I'm agreeing with you."

Blake turned on his heel and faced me. "You're an idiot, do you know that? Or are you just trying to be mean?"

I cleared my throat. "I'm actually not trying to be mean. I'm agreeing. If you aren't interested in men, why does the school have to know that, under some circumstances, you might be?"

He stared at me for a second longer, then pinched the bridge of his nose. "Never mind. Alright, c'mon. We're getting hot dogs. I need some sustenance if I have to deal with your boneheaded behavior."

I wrinkled my nose. "I don't think Kevin the trombonist would've called me a bonehead."

"Kevin the trombonist is a loser and a coward."

"You just don't like him because he wears crocs. Which is rich coming from you and your pizza socks."

"No," Blake snapped, kicking another rock emphatically. "I don't like him because he has a crush on you. And everyone within a mile radius can see it except for you."

I looked up and was surprised to see him scowling. "What do you mean?"

Blake reached the hot dog stand and glared at me for a second before ordering. I said what I wanted and Blake paid.

It was kind of an awkward beat of silence between us as the guy at the stand started to prepare our food.

I broke it by saying, "What do you mean?" again, because Blake had been rude and ignored me.

"I mean he has a crush on you." Blake rolled his eyes and sent me an irritated look. The top of his cheekbones had a tiny flush of red on them. "And that bothers me."

I nodded curtly. "Because you're homophobic."

"No, you idiot," Blake growled. "Because I like you too! How many times do I have to say it? You are seriously the biggest moron I have ever met."

It was weird to hear those words coming from a guy who looked pissed. His electric green eyes were narrowed in on me, his body tense like he was ready for me to hit him. And best of all, he was blushing.

"No way," I scoffed.

"You idiot! I told you that the reason I was mean to that kid when we were younger was because he liked you. I asked you on a date. I held your hand, I cuddled with you for the half-second you let me. I seriously can't think of a single thing that could be any more obvious that all of that."

The guy leaned out of the stand. "Um." He coughed. "Your hot dogs are ready."

I took mine. Blake continued to glare. The hot dog guy just kind of accepted the situation and left the hot dog by the register.

"How could you like me?" I asked, honestly baffled. "We hardly talk."

Blake bit his lip, still glaring. "Just because you suddenly decided you hated me doesn't mean my crush is gonna go away, dude. That's not how it works."

He was making that annoying thing happen to my emotions again.

I felt my heart, actually paying attention to the quickening of it this time, and admitted something that I never thought I would. "I guess I might like you too, Blake. Really deep down. In hell deep down."

"Fine, that's good enough for me."

And then he was leaning towards me, on his tippy toes...

"Jake," Blake snapped. "You're tall. Bend down and kiss me."

He grabbed the back of my neck and I bent down to meet him halfway.

And then, in front of the poor hot dog guy, I kissed my arch nemesis.

Chapter Twelve

W e pulled away from each other and hot dog guy cleared his throat. "Um. Your hot dog is ready."

Blake grabbed the hot dog. "Thanks, we heard you the first fifteen times. Holy shit. C'mon Jake, let's go sit."

I was kind of in a fog of holy shit Blake the snake is a good kisser that was such a good kiss why is my heart beating this fast so I just let him lead me along.

We plopped down across from each other at a picnic table and Blake glared at me. "You aren't saying anything. Why aren't you saying anything? We just kissed, Jake. That has to create some kind of reaction."

I pulled him in and kissed him again.

He gasped a little and accepted the kiss, sending shocks through my body. I curled my hand into his mess of brown hair and guided him closer, surprised at how perfect he felt against me.

He pulled away a little and smiled. "Oh. I thought you'd be mad."

I smiled a little, heart beating fast. "It was an okay kiss."

"You ass."

"...Fine. More than okay. It was..." I searched for a word that was complimentary but would've leave me looking like an idiot. "Good."

His blush came back and he leaned away. "Don't make it weird, okay? I don't usually do this kind of thing with guys. I know you totally hate me and love to make fun of me, you don't have to go all soft now that we kissed."

"Okay," I decided. "You're an idiot."

"Hey!"

"You just kissed me out on the open in front of everyone. What if someone from school is here? There's no way that you checked to make sure everyone is a stranger," I pointed out. "You should've waited until we were in your car before you started demanding kisses from me."

Blake shrugged and gave me a rebellious look. "Maybe I don't care who saw. I like you. I want people to know that."

My heart thumped a little harder and I ate my hot dog I avoid having to respond. I was way too awkward to be hearing these things.

Blake snapped in my face. "Earth to Jake? Do you have an opinion on that?"

Dammit.

I swallowed my hot dog and cleared my throat. "I think that's brave of you. Are you going to come out to the school then?"

Blake shook his head. "No, I'm not going to make some ridiculous announcement. But maybe I'll want to kiss you again, in the hallway. I'm not going to stop myself because of some homophobes."

He was awfully attractive, looking all determined. But no matter how bright his eyes shone with determination, I know I had a say.

"I'm okay with kissing in the hallway," I decided. "I'll feel a little bad for Kevin the trombonist—"

"Fuck Kevin the trombonist."

"—But if that's the way it has to be," I decided. "One thing. I know we're not dating or anything, but please don't kiss women if you're going to be kissing me. I really don't enjoy the thought of second-hand straight people kissing."

Blake looked a little surprised, but then his expression softened. He touched my hand. "I don't want to kiss anybody but you."

I sputtered. "That's not—I didn't mean... weren't we trying to make this not weird? You are awful."

He snorted. "I've never heard you stumble over your words before, dude. Sorry the truth is shocking."

"I don't care who you kiss!"

"Except women."

"Yes. ...And not Gabe either. I know you're newly embracing your gay side, and he's a gay guy at our school, but he's gross and greasy," I demanded. "I don't want to second-hand kiss him either."

Blake looked a little mischievous. "What about Kevin the trombonist?"

"He's scared of you anyway," I scoffed.

"So I can't kiss any women, any gay guys...but I can kiss the straight guys?" Blake's voice sounded teasing.

"They don't want to kiss you, moron. Why would you say that?"

Blake stared at me, amused, for a second. Then he grabbed my hand again. "Like I said before. You don't have to worry about me kissing anyone else, dude."

I decided against arguing. It wasn't that I didn't want him kissing others! I just didn't want to second-hand kiss anybody.

"Whatever," I snapped. "I take it back. Kiss all the women and gay guys you want to."

Blake took a bite of his hot dog and grinned. "How about this. I won't kiss women and gay guys if you don't kiss any other men. Deal?"

I shifted, trying to find a flaw in his logic. But I kind of liked that deal. "Fine."

"But we aren't dating?" Blake asked, taking another innocent bite.

"Don't be ridiculous."

"Okay, Jake," Blake snorted. "Well, dating or not, this was a nice date. We should probably go back now that the sun is heading down though."

I was shocked to feel a little bit of sadness now that our date was coming to a close. I actually wanted to spend more time with Blake? Weird.

I held his hand as we walked back to the car. Before he got in, I got the urge to drop an affectionate kiss onto his forehead. Not one to resist my own urges, I did it.

Blake looked at me with a surprising amount of affection. "Get down here and kiss me, tall guy."

I obeyed the shortass and kissed him against the side of the car. Maybe people were looking, but I wasn't one to care about what others thought.

I pulled away and smiled. "It wasn't unbearable being around you, snake."

Blake pinched my cheek and grinned. "I like you too, douchebag."

Chapter Thirteen

A doorbell ringing startled me and made me choke on my cereal.

"Jake!" my mom screamed. "See who's there!"

It was 6:30 AM, before school, so whoever was there was psychotic.

I opened the door to Blake the snake. Which made sense. He was psychotic sometimes.

"Hey, dude," Blake said. He was wearing sunglasses, a t-shirt even though it was cold, and gray joggers. Horrendous. "I missed you."

Even though his fashion was the worst, my heart stuttered a bit when I saw him.

"You're an idiot," I noted, making him roll his eyes. "Why aren't you wearing a jacket? Come on."

"It's not cold!" Blake whined. "Plus I'm a high school boy, be grateful I'm not wearing basketball shorts right now."

The thought was cringy.

I led him upstairs to my bedroom. He looked around in interest as I fished a sweatshirt out of my closet.

"Wow, this isn't what I expected," Blake noted. "It's messy. Dude, you need to tidy up around here. Want to clean it after school?"

I stuck my head out of the closet and observed. There were a few shirts on the ground, a couple of notebooks, and a few McDonald's wrappers. It was nothing crazy.

"You're anal retentive," I decided. "Here, take this. You're going to be chilly if you don't wear something."

Blake plucked the sweatshirt out of my hands and raised an eyebrow at me. "First you hate me, now you're coddling me? Maybe you're bipolar."

"Don't you like psychology?" I argued. "I'm obviously not."

I grabbed my backpack and looked back at Blake when I realized he hadn't responded. He stared at me. "You actually remembered that?"

He was that shocked that I remembered something. That was... frankly, insulting.

"I know I'm a jock, but I have a few brain cells," I grumbled.

Blake raised a finger. "Highly debatable, dude—" I swung my jacket at him and hit his ass. "Dude!"

He scampered down the stairs and I chased him halfheartedly. "You're an ass," I grumbled. "I have a brain. I also remember things. It's a miracle, I know."

Blake grabbed the sunglasses that had fallen from his head in our little game of chase. "You're a brute. No more shoving me against lockers once we get to school now that we're... kissing. Right?"

I shouldered my backpack and lead us outside. "Fine by me."

"Can I sit next to you in class again?"

"...I guess."

"Can we sit at lunch together?"

I tried my best to stop a smile. "You're pushing it, Beckson."

He shoved me to the side with his hip and smiled. "You're so mean, dude. I'm sitting with you at lunch."

I reached over and grabbed his hand, deciding that I really wouldn't mind if he sat with me and my friends at lunch. "I guess that should be fine. Just don't let Ben talk to you about being my catamite."

Blake shuddered. "Oh trust me, I don't want to hear it."

—//—

Weirdly enough, Blake waved off his friends once we got to school and headed to mine. I had significantly less, and they were weirder, so it was bizarre that Blake actually followed through with his plan to talk to us.

Ben gasped the second he saw us. "Look, guys! Look! What the fuck! Jake is holding his hand! That is so kindergarten of them!"

Unfortunately Ben got the attention of more than my group, so we got a lot of attention from his outburst. Blake shrunk into my arm a little, but I squeezed his hand a little and he straightened up.

I kissed the side of his head and whispered, "Just ignore them. They really don't care at all."

Blake turned his attention on me, eyes wide. "How did you tell people you were gay all by yourself? Even with you here, I'm nervous."

I smirked a little. "I knew I could kick intolerant asses."

Blake rolled his eyes and thankfully we made it to my friends without any sort of commotion. The whole group was looking at us, but Ben was staring. "Guys, like what?" he whispered. "I didn't think your date was going to end successfully."

Blake glared. "And why is that?"

Uh oh. I didn't expect that they wouldn't like each other.

Ben raised an eyebrow. "Well, no duh. Because Jake is emotionally constipated."

Blake snorted. "Okay, that's true."

"Very rude," I told them.

"How awkward was he on your date?" Christi snorted. "Did he even hold your hand? Wait, did he kiss you at the end? Doubt it."

"I had to kiss him," Blake outed me mercilessly. "I also had to hold his hand. And when he played go-carting, he destroyed six year olds emotionally."

Ben grimaced. "I should've warned you about the competitive streak. He's pretty bad. But the go-carting was a good idea then?"

Weirdly, Blake smiled at him. "It was an awesome idea. You're a great wingman."

"Wait!" I interrupted. I pointed at Ben. "You helped him pick out our date? How could you?"

Ben looked smug. "What can I say? I'm a pretty good gay wing man. I think it's my straight guy perspective that brings a new flavor."

Kay rolled her eyes and patted him on the shoulder. "Okay, Ben. We believe you."

"What?!"

Because it was best to not work up Ben, we all headed inside the building as a group ignored his indignant whining.

I squinted at Blake. "You told Ben about the date?"

He blushed. "I wanted advice from your friend and, ya know, another other gay guy. To make the date good."

I couldn't stop my own smile. "That was—"

"Excuse me?!" Ben sputtered.

Blake and Ben began bickering, so I focused on my two girl friends to give them details of my date.

And I pointedly ignored the fact that we were surround by people whispering to each other.

Chapter Fourteen

I despised people for many reasons. One, they breathed. Two, they had opinions. Three, sometimes their opinions hurt others.

I could tell that Blake wasn't fully comfortable with holding my hand in the hallway.

The reason being, many people in our school seemed shocked that he would do such a thing. It didn't seem to be about him holding hands with a guy. It was about him.

On more than one occasion, I heard someone gasp and say, "Not Blake?!"

A few others wondered what his ex-girlfriend would say.

Some speculated which positions we were in bed.

And everything that was said was whispered loud enough to be audible. And Blake's bravado was wavering.

While Ms. Nelson droned on in our statistics class, Blake turned to me with uncertainty in his eyes. "Psst. Dude," he whispered. "Everyone is talking about me."

I gave him a shaky grin. "They're mad because you're hot and the girls think you're only into guys."

He rolled his eyes. "That's some bull. They hate me now."

I squeezed his hand. "That's not true, Blake. Trust me, this school is obsessed with you. They're just shocked. Just wait, tomorrow nobody will be saying anything."

He grimaced. "I'm scared about lunch period. I don't want them to say they hate me."

I bit my lip, slightly worried. It was weird to feel nervous on behalf of somebody else's feelings, but I was. I didn't want to see his feelings hurt. I wanted him to be happy, especially because I'd played a part in motivating him to come out.

I kind of wanted to beat up everyone who sent him a second glance.

"Boys, quiet," Ms. Nelson snapped.

Maybe I could just beat up Ms. Nelson.

By the time lunch rolled around, Blake was freaking out. He grabbed at my locker and groaned. "I can't do it. I'm gonna get pushed in the lunch line. Someone's gonna spill spaghetti sauce on me!"

I patted his head and grabbed my lunchbox. "You'll be fine."

"You're not comforting, dude!" Blake whined. "Make me feel better. Reassure me!"

He was absolutely resorting to being melodramatic because it was easier than being scared.

I kissed his forehead. Shockingly, the tension in his shoulders dissipated slightly.

"Your friends god-worship you, Blake," I reminded him. "It was one of the many reasons why I hated you." He glared. "I know you'll be alright."

Except I didn't know that at all.

Blake sat down with my friend group at lunch, which wasn't the best thing he could've done to protect his feelings.

Kay raised an eyebrow. "Wow. I thought you were too cool to sit here," she drolly commented.

Kay thought she was badass. In order to support this, she would occasionally pretend like she was more mean than she actually was.

Blake shifted awkwardly. "I never thought I was too cool. I just wasn't invited."

I pet his head. "Don't worry, she's not serious. She likes to pretend that she's a mean person when she actually isn't."

Blake's eyes narrowed. "Are you serious?"

Kay shrugged and opened her pudding. "Maybe, maybe not."

"See," Christi groaned. "She's not that cool. But if you go along with it, you'll be fine."

Kay elbowed her.

The conversation was calm in the three minutes that Ben wasn't there, but the second he sat down he brought trouble.

"So!" Ben began. "Blakey boy. When did you decide that being Jake's catamite is the lifestyle that's right for you?"

Blake coughed. "Jake told me not to answer those kinds of questions."

Ben shoved his finger in my face. "J! Why are you always such a buzzkill? So what if I want to talk to your new boyfriend a little?"

"He's not my new boyfriend," I grumbled.

Christi blinked. "Um. How? You guys are all cuddly."

"We're not officially dating though," Blake explained.

"But you are together?" Kay asked.

"No," I said.

"Yes," Blake said.

We looked at each other.

"It's complicated," I decided.

Blake nodded.

Thankfully, someone interrupted our slightly awkward conversation. I recognized Kelly, who sat next to Blake in English.

She sent Blake a bitchy look. "Why aren't you sitting at our table? Are you mad at us? Because that would be rich."

Blake nibbled on his bottom lip. "I wanted to sit with Jake?"

"What?" she snapped. "Because you're butt buddies now? Asshole, you're being a traitor to your friends."

Of course Ben had popcorn in his lunchbox. He popped one into his mouth and hummed. "Mm, drama."

Blake glared at him. "Why am I being an asshole that I want to sit with my almost-boyfriend?"

My heart hurt so badly from his poor grammar, I almost missed the almost-boyfriend part.

"Because! You're ditching us," Kelly snapped. "First you keep secrets, then you don't talk to any of us all day, and now you're ditching us. Are you like mad or something?"

Blake fidgeted. "No? I thought you guys would hate me for being bisexual."

Kelly gestured in a frustrated way. "Blake, I'm bisexual."

Blake fidgeted. "I know... but I didn't want Alana do be upset or anything."

Ah. Alana. That was his ex-girlfriend.

Judging by the way Blake was nibbling on his lip and shifting nervously, he cared about stupid Alana's opinion.

I wanted to leave.

This conversation was now very boring to me.

Kelly scoffed. "Alana doesn't mind! Blake, you're so dumb sometimes. Come back to our table, you'll see. We love you, nobody cares."

Relief reduced the tension in Blake's shoulders and a smile appeared. It was nice to me to see him happy after being nervous all day, but I wasn't happy that stupid Alana was the reason.

"Okay, I'll go back," traitor Blake said. "I'll see you later?"

Oh. He was talking to me.

I shrugged. "Yeah, see you on the walk home."

Blake looked like he wanted to say something else, or maybe do something else, but he walked away.

I shoved my sandwich in my mouth and pretended like I didn't want him to turn around.

Chapter Fifteen

B y the time I saw Blake again, it was after school and he was beaming.

"Have a good talk with Alana?" I asked, trying to ignore my own irritation. If Blake wanted to talk to his ex, fine.

If Blake's ex gave him more comfort than I did, fine.

Luckily, I must have hidden it well. "Yeah!" he chirped. He was buried inside of my giant sweatshirt with the track team's logo on it. He honestly looked adorable. "She's not mad."

Blake reached out and took my hand, and I kind of wanted to ignore it to be petty. But I wasn't petty, I was a nice person, so I took it.

"Why would she be mad?" I wondered.

"Because I lied to her," Blake sounded stressed. "And I broke up with her recently because of you. But I told her that and she wasn't even upset, she told me that she wanted me to find love!"

Sounded like Alana wasn't into him in the first place. What a bitch.

"She sounds nice," I gritted out. "I'm glad today went well."

Something broke Blake out of his happy-go-lucky disposition and he sent me a look. "Dude, are you okay? You sound grumpy."

"I'm always grumpy."

"I know, but more than usual." He chewed on his pinky nail a little and then blurted out, "Hey I don't wanna be, like, weird, but are you mad at me?"

"Nope."

"Jake!" He pulled away and glared. I was glad that we were a ways from school so nobody could see the scene he was causing. "Do you mind actually talking to me?"

Great. We weren't even dating yet and he was mad at me.

"I'm fine," I muttered, because I honestly wasn't sure why I was grumpy. "I'm actually happy for you."

That was true.

"Then what the hell?"

"I don't know!" I admitted. "I just...I don't know. I don't know. I'm as confused as you are."

He leveled me with a curious stare and then hummed. He took my hand and we kept walking. "Okay. When did these negative emotions begin?"

"...Are you playing therapist right now?"

"Shh, Jake. Tell me."

It didn't take me too long to remember when they started. "When you were worried about stupid Alana."

"At lunch?"

"Yes," I muttered. "And you scampered off to go talk to stupid Alana."

He was grinning now, not that I had any idea why. "Oh? What else?"

"And now you're all happy, because stupid Alana gave you her stupid approval." I scoffed. "I just don't get why you're so hung up on her."

He elbowed me teasingly and poked my cheek. "It's okay if you're jealous, dude. But I don't have feelings for Alana anymore. I told you, I broke up with her because I like you."

That gave me way too much reassurance.

"I'm not jealous," I scoffed. "That's ridiculous. We aren't even together." Actually, that reminded me that Blake had answered yes when we were asked that question at lunch. "...Are we together?"

Blake shrugged and put his annoying cool kid sunglasses on. "I dunno, dude. I thought so. I mean I know you don't want to be my boyfriend or anything, but I thought we were exclusive."

"Exclusive? What are we, eighty-five years old?" I deadpanned.

"Dude! That's a thing. Remember when we agreed not to kiss anyone else? Or, you know, do other things?" Blake asked, blush creeping onto his cheeks. "That's exclusive. We're together."

I really liked that idea. Now that I realized Blake wasn't a homophobe, it was clear to me that he had been right. He was my type. Physically, for sure. But also mentally. He was a nice person. He was dorky and cute and a little awkward, but also honest and caring.

Way too caring, where stupid Alana was concerned.

"I like you, I think," I admitted. "Which is weird, but okay. You're a good kisser. We went on a fun date."

Blake looked at me, eyes shining with happiness. "Do you want to be my boyfriend?"

"No, that wasn't what I was saying at all."

His shoulders slumped and he kicked at a rock. "Oh."

"How will we know if we're compatible unless we go through adversity together?" I thought, making Blake roll his eyes and wrinkle his nose. "Being my boyfriend implies forever. That's a lot of pressure considering we were at each other's throats five seconds ago."

Blake crossed his arms. "Dude, we're in high school. It doesn't have to be all forever like. It can just be casual."

I wasn't okay with casual. Being a boyfriend meant being emotionally vulnerable. Any person who got to see me emotionally vulnerable was going to die by my side.

Ahem. In a married, in-love-forever, kind of way.

And then I had a horrific vision of dying at the age of 80, and Blake at my funeral saying, "Dudes, he was like kinda grumpy."

I cleared my throat. "Maybe we shouldn't be boyfriends."

Blake groaned. "Jake! I like you. You like me. What more do we need?"

A good eulogy.

"Um, I think we need to see how compatible we are first," I blurted out, trying to shake the weird existential vision of my own funeral out of my head. "Maybe an escape room?"

He made a face. "What?"

"We should do an escape room together. Tonight. That way we can see how well we work together under pressure. You know, compatibility," I explained. "If we're going to be boyfriends, we need to be good together."

He hummed. "Alana never thought this much into things."

I was beginning to get a headache. "Oh look, it's our houses thank God. Now I don't have to listen to you saying stupid Alana's name anymore."

Blake snorted and elbowed me again. "You're so cute when you're jealous."

I groaned and ignored how my face started to feel awfully warm. "Escape room or not?"

"Fine, I'm in. I just have to eat dinner first," he said. "Then we'll go."

I extended my hand to shake on it, which made Blake roll his eyes. "Dude, I'm not going to seal the deal with a handshake. Kiss me."

Against my permission or wishes, my heart thudded a little faster. Blake Beckson looked alluring, with determination in his eyes and his lips pressed together in a slight pout.

I ran my fingers through his soft, wavy hair, and I leaned in.

This kiss was a thousand times better than the first, without the presence of a hot dog guy or my own nerves. I kissed him like I wanted him to remember it for years. And he was just as passionate, getting up on his tippy toes to be as close as possible.

When he pulled away, he smirked. "We'll be compatible."

And for the first time in the history of walking home from school with Blake Beckson, he went inside his house and I wanted him to stay with me longer.

Chapter Sixteen

We weren't the only ones in the escape room, which kind of ruined the low-key fantasies I had of making out with Blake against a puzzle-covered table.

"This is stupid," Blake declared.

I rolled my eyes. "It's not stupid. We need to find out if we can solve problems together. Maybe we should ask the family that's going in with us to not contribute."

"Can I say something?" Blake whined. "I have an opinion on your whole problem solving thing. I kind of feel like the ability to work together as a couple and solve problems is something that two people figure out over time in their relationship, as they—"

"Excuse me?" I asked the dad of the family. "Do you and your children mind not contributing to the escape room?"

Blake turned around and hit his head against the wall dramatically. "Holy shit."

The older guy wrinkled his nose. "Why? That would be a waste of money, don't you think?"

That was a fair point. "In the spirit of romance?" I attempted. "This is my potential boyfriend, Blake. Sorry he has his head against the wall, he's embarrassed by me right now. We're doing this escape room to see if we should become a couple."

The mother looked at Blake with something similar to pity in her eyes. "That seems like a...nontraditional way of going about things."

"What, a boy having a boyfriend?" I asked, prepared for it.

"...No, honey. Why is the escape room deciding if you'll be good for each other?" she asked, pulling her toddler son closer to her legs. Why even bring a toddler to an escape room?

"I'm happy to explain."

"No, he isn't going to explain," Blake interrupted, pulling me away a little. "I'm so sorry. You can totally contribute. He's just a weirdo."

The family moved farther away from us. "Blake, what the heck?"

"Why are you so weird?" he groaned. "You're such an oddball. Dude, they paid. We're just gonna do the escape room and beat it and then you'll be my boyfriend, right?"

Wait, were those the standards? I didn't realize that this was the final determining factor.

"Noooo," I corrected. "This will help me find out if we should date."

Blake pouted and shoved his head into my arm. "Why won't you date me, dude? Kiss me." I kissed him. "See? We're already at kissing level!"

"Kissing is one thing," I said. "Emotional vulnerability is another."

He stared at me blankly before groaning. "You're such a typical man."

Now that was offensive.

"Excuse me?!"

"You know," Blake said, shrugging. "Afraid of crying, speaking in anything other than monotone, and emotional vulnerability."

The mom of the family seemed to be nodding along.

"Aren't you insulting yourself?!" I sputtered.

"Nope," Blake chirped. "I'd be emotionally vulnerable with you. Actually, I already have been."

Huh. He was turning this into a competition.

That changed things.

"Alright, everybody!" an employee cut in before I could respond. "For the next 60 minutes, you'll be working together with the folks around you to...escape."

He said it in a dramatic tone, like it wasn't exactly what we were all expecting.

"I'm your game guide, Erwin. I'm going to take you inside our escape room, where we will watch a video that explains your mission. Everyone follow me."

We all followed dweeby peppy Erwin into a dimly lit room with a TV. Erwin chattered off some boring rules and expectations, as well as explained what an escape room even was. Erwin definitely thought we were all stupid.

Then he began the video. Apparently, Blake, the family, and I were all really bad thieves. In an attempt to steal a priceless artifact, we tripped an alarm system and only had 60 minutes to escape.

"Mommy, I'm scared," the toddler mumbled.

"It's okay, Carl."

What kind of toddle was named Carl? This family was weird.

Erwin informed us that he would be watching us over cameras and ready to assist at moments notice.

And finally, finally, we were in.

"Ooh, dudes, this place is sick!" Blake exclaimed.

"Wow!" Carl said.

"Nice to know the children of the group are on the same page," I deadpanned, getting a hard stomach slap from Blake.

It was kind of cool. The room was decorated to look like a museum, completed with statue busts and interesting paintings. There were a few random puzzles dispersed throughout the room, which I figured we'd be forced to solve to win.

"Alright, we're on the clock!" Dad yelled. "Let's get moving."

"So would it be futile to ask you to not participate again?" I questioned.

He glared. "Get moving."

Twenty minutes later, the only thing that had been solved was the magnetic puzzle on the wall. And sadly, it was solved by Carl. How the kid managed to figure it out was beyond me, he was like three. And too short to reach most of the puzzle.

Blake and I were arguing over a Sudoku puzzle on the wall.

"It's a three there," I snapped. Blake elbowed me.

"We already tried three, blockhead! It's a five, look, it lines up right there," Blake said. He played around with the numbers a little until it became evident that the five and the three both didn't work. "Okay, we need to work together."

Ah. It's almost like the escape room was teaching us how to problem-solve! Knew it.

"I have a plan. Why don't we start with this first square and try to fill in the numbers that add to ten," I said, pointing to the square. "We can start with the numbers that aren't in the square."

"And with each number we can cross the rows and columns out if they have it, because they can only be used once!" Blake said.

Our eyes met and it was a moment of comradery. I couldn't resist the urge to kiss his nose.

"Ew!" Carl said.

When his parents weren't looking, I flipped him off.

After a few minutes, we finished up the Sudoku puzzle. I wrapped Blake up in an affectionate, but not inappropriate-for-Carl affectionate, hug. "We did it. See, we might be compatible."

Blake laughed this time instead of getting annoyed. "Maybe you're right. C'mon, let's do the huge freaking knot over there."

We struggled at first, and Carl told us that we sucked. I flipped him off again.

By the end of the 60 minutes, Carl had completed four problems, Blake and I finally were done with the knot, and Carl's parent's hadn't noticed the five times I had flipped off their irritating son.

"You're an asshole!" Carl told me before his family walked away.

Carl's mom gasped. "Carl!"

Carl's dad rolled his eyes. "He kind of was, Karen."

"Bill!"

"So how did that go?" Blake asked me as we walked back to the car. "Do you feel like we're compatible? Are our problem-solving skills up to par?"

I didn't even realize I was smiling until I sat in the front seat and saw myself in the mirror. "Sub-par. The dick bag three year old finished double the amount of puzzles that we did."

"True, but at least we aren't dick bags," Blake snorted.

I grabbed his hand as we drove away and kissed it. "We're pretty good together, Beckson. Maybe we would be a good couple."

Blake gave me an expectant look and the vision of my funeral came back.

This time, Blake had his earbuds in as everyone buried me. "I kind of liked him, dudes, but he flipped off a three year old once!"

I shuttered. "One more date?"

Blake gave me a determined look. "Tomorrow."

"Tomorrow it is."

Chapter Seventeen

At school the next day, I was approached by stupid Alana. "Hi Jake," she began. "I know you don't really like talking to people, but can we talk?"

One point for recognizing my antisocial tendencies.

One point lost for not respecting them.

Alana was a classically pretty girl. Dark hair, dark eyes, kind of a hippie style. She wore flowers and ripped jeans and owned a shoulder bag instead of a backpack. Very cool.

"Yes," I said, simply because I had no idea what she would want from me and I was curious.

"So I know you and Blake are dating," she said, which wasn't accurate. "And I just want you to know that it totally doesn't have to be awkward around us! I knew Blake fell out of love with me a long time ago, and I didn't want to admit it. Now, we're both in better places."

I really did not know what to say.

"We've never spoken before," I reminded her.

She nodded, brown eyes wide and sweet. "I know."

"Well, I don't see why we'd be speaking in the future then." I shrugged. "Mutual ignoring isn't awkward to me."

And then I walked away.

That was weird.

Blake met up with me around lunchtime, looking bothered. "Were you mean to Alana?"

I snorted. "Are you on stupid Alana's side now?"

Blake's friends were waving at him obnoxiously, which only made me more irritated. Blake saw them and smiled. "Jake, I gotta go, okay? We can talk later!"

I plopped down at my table and Ben pet my head. "I'm sorry, my man," Ben sighed. "I can tell that you and your catamite are having troubles."

"We're not," I huffed, taking a bite of apple to avoid talking.

Christi sat next to me. "Hey Jake, why so sad? Because Gabe is eyeballing your man?"

"What?" I scanned the lunchroom for Gabe and sure enough he was totally undressing my potential boyfriend with his eyes.

Kay hummed. "Oh yeah. Gabe's into him alright. If you hadn't been so pissed at nothing yesterday, you would've heard the rumors."

This was the worst day of my life. "What rumors?"

I really did not want to know.

Ben happily told me. "Gabe wants to ask Blake to prom."

I was going to beat up Gabe.

"Blake is my prom date," I snapped.

"You asked him?" Christi yelled. "And you didn't even say anything about it?"

"How could you betray me like this!" Ben was adding onto the drama. "Not in the way where I was expecting to be asked, because I'm not gay, but like you didn't tell me important details of your life?!"

Kay just sighed. "You and Ben would've looked so good in blue."

Ben hit her shoulder.

"I didn't ask him," I admitted, getting a whole bunch of eye rolls from my friend group. "It's just obvious. Who am I supposed to go with, Kevin the trombonist?"

Until now, I had been planning on going alone. Or better yet, not at all. But the idea of Gabe with Blake was enough to set my blood on fire.

"If you didn't ask him, Gabe can," Kay chided. "Don't be dense."

I had been so dense.

I had been so busy being jealous over Alana yesterday that I didn't realize the situation. Blake was now openly available to everyone.

Except the straight boys, but whatever.

Of course Blake would have a date to prom! He was handsome, funny, kind, and very popular. And now officially free game to everyone at school.

"I'm going to ask him then," I decided. "Like, right now."

"Well, hurry," Kay laughed. "Gabe's already up."

Wait what?

Sure enough, greasy Gabe had already made it all the way to Blake and was tapping on his shoulder.

I leapt up and hustled over to the table.

"Blake?" greasy Gabe said in his cocky voice. "Would you like to go to prom with me?"

I bodied Gabe out of the way and faced my potential boyfriend. "Blake! Prom?" I glared at Gabe.

Blake choked on his yogurt.

"Hey!" slimy Gabe stood up from the ground, oops, and he shoved a finger in my face. "I'm asking him!"

I looked down at him. I observed his tiny frame. I observed my frame of hulking muscle. "Are you trying to fight me?" I asked honestly.

It was hard to tell with scrawny people.

Greasy Gabe gasped. "No, please don't hurt me!" Once he realized that I wasn't going to, he looked at Blake again. "Would you want to—"

I pushed him by the head and he toppled.

"Don't listen to the weasel," I snapped. "I want to be your date to prom."

Blake scowled. "Stop being violent."

I sighed and gave Gabe a hand to help him off the ground. Gabe took it shakily and leapt away from me once he was on his feet.

"Blake!" Gabe cried. "You know I've had a crush on you forever. I just—"

I faced him. "Do you want to end up on the ground again?"

He took a step back and held up his hands. "No, Jake. Please don't hurt me. I just think you're not meant for Blake."

"I think that's Blake's choice to decide," I said, giving him a pointed look.

Blake raised an eyebrow. "Oh, is that why you shoved him to the ground twice?"

I shrugged. "I had to show my dominance."

Blake laughed. Ha. Point for me.

I faced Gabe. "Come on, Gabe. What sounds better, Gabe and Blake? Or Jake and Blake? Let's be logical. Our names rhyme."

"That means nothing!"

I turned back to Blake. "Want to go for prom king and king? I think we might win, with your popularity and my brutal competitive streak."

Blake folded his arms over his chest and glared. "Is you not letting Gabe take me to prom part of your competitive streak?"

"No," I admitting, feeling a little self-conscious of all the eyes on us. "It's because there's nobody else I'd rather go with."

And then I was kissing Blake Beckson, my former arch nemesis, in the middle of the lunchroom.

Blake pulled away and smiled. "Sorry, Gabe. I think I want to take Jake to prom."

Chapter Eighteen

I was feeling good about going to prom with Blake. Actually, I couldn't stop smiling.

It creeped people out, because I wasn't known for being visibly cheery. In fact, there was a rumor floating around that my facial muscles were paralyzed.

In English, we were lucky enough to get time to work with our partners. Blake and I sat next to each other and worked diligently on our project.

"Jake, stop texting," Blake said for what seemed like the millionth time. "We need to finish the project, dude."

He cared so much about school. It was so annoying.

I put my phone away. "My mom's going to freak out now that I stopped texting. The deaths that her panic causes are on your hands."

Blake rolled his eyes and propped his feet up on my lap. "She'll be fine. So we have our textual analysis. We have potential thematic topics. Now we need to pick one, then make a thesis out of it."

A random girl tapped my shoulder and leaned in. "You guys are such a cute couple! What color are you going to wear to prom?"

I wrinkled my nose. "Aren't tuxedos black?"

The girl bounced in her chair a little. "Can you wear the colors of your pride flags? I think it would be so cute!"

Would that make me rainbow?

"No," I chose wisely. "I won't be doing that."

"I'm considering buying bisexual themed graphic t-shirts, if that makes you feel better," Blake offered.

She grinned. "That works too!"

"Anyway," Blake grumbled. "Which thematic topic do you want to do?"

"That one," I said, pointing at cyclical nature of life without honestly knowing what the hell that meant.

"Awesome!" Blake honestly just seemed happy that I was contributing. "Let's come up with—"

"So guys," Christi leaned in. "Are you both wearing tuxedos? Because I honestly think Jake would look hot in a dress."

I grimaced. "I'm gay, Christi. There's no room for dresses in this relationship."

"Hey Jake!" Kevin the trombonist called. He sent me a toothy smile. "It was really cool of you, what you did at lunch. I think I might ask someone later today." He sent Gabe a lustful look.

They would be perfect for each other.

"Good for you, Kevin," I said. "I'm sure whoever it is would love to go with you."

Dr. Clark cleared her throat. "Why the chatter today? Are you all focused on your schoolwork?"

Random girl's hand shot up. "It's a big day, Dr. Clark. Jake is a gay icon!"

Dr. Clark blinked. "I'm sorry?"

"He asked Blake to prom!"

Dr. Clark suddenly looked more human than robot. "Oh, wow! Congratulations, boys. That's very nice."

Blake sunk low into his seat. "Thank you, ma'am."

I shrugged. "To be fair, it was Gabe's idea."

I pointed at Gabe and the kid looked away like I was going to beat him up.

Dr. Clark brightened. "Good on you, Gabe, for encouraging your friend to do such a thing!"

Gabe flinched. "Thanks, ma'am."

We didn't bother correcting her.

After everyone resumed their work, random girl attacked again.

"So when did you two start dating?" she asked. "I honestly thought you guys hated each other. I mean, Jake talked about how much he hated Blake every single day."

I cleared my throat. "I had a change of heart. He's not the worst."

She leaned in. "So...not to be too nosy, but are you guys...doing stuff?"

"Michaela!" Blake sputtered.

Oh. That was her name.

"What?! I'm just curious! You don't have to tell me, but I had to ask," she gushed. "Since Ben went around saying everything about catamites, I figured sex would be on the table for you two."

I rotated in my chair until my gaze settled on Ben. I glared.

He grinned. "You guys should bang!"

Blake dropped his head to the desk. "This is sexual harassment."

I flipped Ben off.

Dr. Clark cleared her throat. "Boys, I know it's an exciting day for you, but the chatter has to stop over there."

"Sorry!" I piped up, glad to have a distraction from the conversation.

Blake leaned in as everyone resumed their work. "Um, do you want to have sex?"

What the hell?

I stared at him. "Where did that come from?"

He flushed. "I mean if you were telling Ben that you want to have sex with me..." He trailed off and shrugged. "I've never done that with a boy, but..."

I pinched the bridge of my nose. "I'm going to kill Ben. I wasn't going around saying that."

"It kind of seems like it, since everyone knows, so—"

"I wasn't," I growled.

Blake blinked a little and hurt flashed across his features. "So you don't want to? I get it. That's not...offensive or anything."

Now he was upset? And just a few minutes ago we'd been gay icons.

"Blake," I stressed. "I'm not calling you ugly or unattractive. I'm just saying...something like that is for someone important, you know? I've never had sex with a man either. I'm not just going to throw that out the window with anybody."

Blake looked at me like I'd slapped him. "Seriously?"

"What?" I sputtered. "That's how I feel. I'm being honest. Why is honesty a crime?"

He bit his bottom lip and dropped his gaze to his paper. "Let's just finish the project."

"Blake—"

"Can we just finish already?" he snapped. He glared at me and I remembered how intense those green eyes of his were when he was angry. "I'm getting sick and tired of your lack of academic motivation."

Well, that was the nerdiest sentence ever.

Because he was clearly upset, I decided to shut up and do my work.

I figured Blake would be over it by the time we walked home together, but after waiting outside school for five minutes too long, someone had informed me that he'd started walking without me.

So much for our date tonight.

It was kind of lonely to walk without Blake. For the first time, I began to realize just how much I liked having him around.

Chapter Nineteen

I knocked on the door of Blake's house at 6-way-too-early o'clock, feeling desperate.

Blake hadn't answered any of my texts. And for a guy who was kind of obsessed with me, and who was also going to be my date to prom, this was weird behavior.

Blake answered his door wearing gym shorts and no shirt. I tried my best not to let my eyes wander, but it was hard.

He was shirtless! And he had such nice, lean muscles. And his sharp hip-bones disappeared into the too-low shorts, creating a V that was difficult to stop staring at.

He scowled. "Oh. So now I'm sexually attractive."

And then he slammed the door in my face.

I deserved that.

I knocked again. "Blake, please answer. I miss you. ...And honestly that was a difficult thing to admit, so please open the door."

He opened the door.

He was so attractive. I had no idea why he thought I thought otherwise.

Really, nobody in the world looked like Blake Beckson. He was a mix of innocent and sexy. His curly brown hair gave him a boyish charm, but the strength of his jaw turned me on. The muscled curve of his shoulders was a contrast to the soft kindness I could see in his green eyes.

Heat burned on my cheeks. "You're beautiful, Blake," I admitted. "And so, so attractive. If I made you feel like I didn't believe that, I'm sorry."

"Aww!" Blake's mom popped up from behind him. "Blake!"

Blake waved her away, face red. "Mom! Please give us some privacy."

She drifted away after giving me a wink.

"It's not that," Blake said. His stern tone wasn't exactly convincing, with the deep red blush on his cheeks. "You said that...you implied that I wasn't important. Which is fine. I just don't think we should bother trying to be together anymore if that's what you think."

My heart sunk in my chest at his words and the determination in his eyes. "You don't really mean that, right?"

He nodded.

"I know I wasn't really gung ho about us at first, but our last date..." I looked at Blake, trying to figure out what had changed. "You have to admit, we had something special. We were almost better than the three year old!"

I almost got him to smile.

Part of me was remembering what Blake had said that night, about being emotionally vulnerable. If he could be emotionally vulnerable, so could I.

Without realizing it, I'd become attached to Blake. He became important to me. I wanted him in my life.

Part of me knew, even though I didn't want to admit it, that I wanted him as my boyfriend. All the jealousy I felt from Gabe helped me realize it.

But Blake was glaring at me, so I'd be emotionally vulnerable some other time.

Blake cleared his throat and looked at the ground. "You aren't as into me as I'm into you. I honestly just think we need time apart. Maybe...maybe we can have a ten foot distance between us when we walk to school, so people don't see us and think we're friends."

What a rude fucking concept that was. I tried not to be indignant.

"I guess I'll get walking, then," I muttered, turning away and trying to ignore the twisted feeling in my chest.

My friends at school didn't make me feel better. In fact, they kept bringing him up.

Christi nudged me at lunchtime, a shit-eating grin on her face. "So did you and Blake do the do? I heard that girl Michaela talking to you two."

I tried to ignore the way my heart squeezed.

"No," I said gruffly, turning and walking to my locker.

I caught sight of Blake leaning up against stupid Alana's locker. She laughed and twirled her hair.

Nope.

I was way too into Blake to let that happen.

I appeared by Blake's right shoulder and tapped him. "Hi. Can we talk? Again?"

Alana looked at me and suddenly got this weirdly awkward look on her face. I had no idea why.

"I'll leave you two," Alana said. She walked off before we could say anything.

"No, wait—ugh." Blake pinched the bridge of his nose and gave me that look again. The mostly angry, but definitely still hurt, look. "Jake. C'mon. Remember the distance?"

Fuck the distance.

"I'm an idiot," I exclaimed. "I shouldn't have said what I said."

Blake blushed and looked at the group of people who were staring at us. Wait, when had that happened?

"We can talk about this later—"

"No, fuck that," I scoffed, determined to make things right. "I know why you're mad at me. I know I implied that you weren't important to me. But that's not what I meant!"

Blake crossed his arms and leaned against the locker. I tried not to get distracted by his biceps. "Then what did you mean?"

"I mean we need to be closer to have—" Right, the crowd of people. "—to do that. I want you to be my real boyfriend before we do that, because I want it to be special."

There. For the first time, I felt like I'd communicated my emotions well.

It was a big day.

Then someone whispered, "Damn, did you hear that, Angela? They didn't bang."

I turned my attention back to Blake. Surprisingly, he wasn't glaring. He was staring at me like I'd grown a third head—eyes wide and mouth parted.

"So you're actually willing to try this?" Blake asked, amazed. "You don't secretly hate me still? Or you aren't having some weird competition with Gabe?"

I tugged him closer to me by his waist and our foreheads touched. "I like you, Blake. A lot. I know you said we're together, but I want to become your boyfriend... after some more research into our compatibility. I want to take you to prom. Would you like to go on another date?"

He smiled at me and his beautiful green eyes filled with delight. "Hell yeah, dude. Let's do it."

I kissed him and the crowd fell away. That is, until Angela whispered, "Aw!" and the hallway filled with soft noises that people usually made at puppies.

The second Blake and I pulled apart, everyone busied themselves with their bags as if they hadn't been staring.

I looked at Blake to gauge his reaction, but he just smiled and held my hand.

And in that moment, I made myself a promise. Blake Beckson would be my boyfriend.

Chapter Twenty

"Alright, dude, will you be my boyfriend after this date?" Blake asked, borderline whining. "We kissed, we problem-solved, and we even fought for the first time. We're ready."

I stared at the breakfast place like it had the answers to all of my problems. "...Maybe."

"Dude! You were even emotionally vulnerable," Blake sighed. He ran a hand through his brown hair in frustration. "You're seriously backing out now?"

I wanted Blake to be my boyfriend. I knew that in my heart.

But still, it was hard to be so accepting! For one, I'd never had a boyfriend. But it was also Blake the snake we were talking about!

...Okay, no, I liked Blake a lot. That wasn't a reason. Old habits die hard.

"I didn't like being emotionally vulnerable," I muttered. "I was jealous because of Alana, jealous because of Gabe, guilty because of how I treated you, but hurt that you pushed me away...that's a lot of emotions at once, Beckson! Too many."

Blake pinched the bridge of his nose. "Dude, if you're disinterested in feeling emotions, we're gonna have to turn these dates into therapy sessions."

In past experiences, or really, one past experience, I had not enjoyed Therapist Blake™.

"No thank you, I'll feel emotion," I promised. "Let's just go on in."

Finally, after our twenty minute long conversation, we entered the diner. It was filled with old people and the smell of pancakes, two of my least favorite things.

And yet, I held Blake's hand and the whole experience wasn't so negative.

I still had to complain though. Complaints were my life energy.

"I hate pancakes," I muttered. "...And old people."

Blake took a look around. "So this is not the place for you, dude. No worries, we'll order eggs or something."

An old lady walked up to us with a smile. ...Wait, this was a familiar old lady. "Nancy?" I asked. "From our neighborhood?"

She was the one with the trash can. And the cookies.

Nancy brightened. "Oh, hello boys! I'm here to get you two seated. Are you out on a little date today?"

We both were silent for a few seconds before I answered, "Yes. In fact, this date determines if we'll be boyfriends."

Nancy wrinkled her nose. "Well, that's a very non-traditional way of doing things. Shouldn't coming together be...natural?"

Blake rolled his eyes. "This is Jake we're talking about. I'm just lucky that this morning isn't a test of our conversational compatibility or something."

Rude.

Fair, but rude.

Nancy laughed and guided us to a table. "Well, here you are." She winked. "I hope the date goes well."

I shuttered after she walked away. "That was a lot of old person all at once. Gross."

"So we need to talk about yesterday," Blake blurted out.

I did not want to reflect on my moment of assholery. "I'd rather we didn't." At Blake's look, I gave in. "What specifically do you want to talk about?"

Blake looked around and then leaned in. "Okay, so I have some clarifying questions. One, you're a virgin?"

"Obviously."

"Okay, cool. I'm a butt virgin." The worst part about that sentence was how sincerely Blake said it. "So...you said yesterday that you want me to become important--"

"No, you are important," I added. "I just meant that I want us to be official before we go...exposing ourselves like that. Physically and emotionally."

Blake rolled his eyes. "Okay, okay. Got it. But you said that you want me to become important. Does that mean that you want to have sex with me eventually?"

This was a dangerous question.

Because on one hand, no shit I wanted to have sex with Blake. Blake was sex on legs. He was, as he once mentioned, exactly what I wanted in a man physically.

But on the other hand, part of me expected Straight Blake™ to come back and be revolted at the idea of sex with me.

I wiggled in my chair. "Well. I want to...you should know this, I want to be your boyfriend. Eventually. And if that were to happen, hypothetically, we'd have hypothetical sex, right?"

Blake deadpanned. "Hot."

This was the worst. "Don't be sarcastic, you're the one mentioning awkward topics. You're lucky I'm not judging our conversational compatibility."

Blake leaned in even further. "I'm just saying--"

Nancy came back to take our drink order. I tried not to roll my eyes. We ordered our drinks.

Blake leaned in again. "Dude, I want us to date too. And I just needed to know that you'd want to have sex with me before that, because I have every intention of having sex with you."

Even though it was the world's most uncomfortable breakfast topic, I couldn't help but feel a little turned on at that. And, partially, a little wooed.

"Aren't we jumping a little bit into the future, though?" I asked, trying to backtrack away from the conversation and the weird emotions it gave me. "I mean, we aren't even dating."

Blake glared at me, green eyes determined, and he leaned in for a kiss. And I stopped saying whatever I was saying, because Blake wanting a kiss was far more important.

We pulled away, only slightly. "Says the guy who wanted to make sure we were able to problem solve."

"That's important!"

"That's excessive," Blake snorted. "Besides, we will be dating. Today. And then we'll go to prom together in the spring. Does that sound like a plan?"

I was blushing for sure. This was humiliating. "You're really that certain?"

Blake nodded.

And I was scared, for sure, but I wanted to date him so badly that it didn't matter. All my insecurities about Alana or Gabe, or anyone else who saw Blake as attractive, disappeared. My worries about emotional vulnerability did as well. Any thoughts of Blake suddenly turning back into Straight Blake™ went away in a hurry as he leaned in to kiss me again.

"Well, screw it," I decided. "I want you to be my boyfriend, Blake the snake. I think you're cute now, unlike before."

Blake shook his head, half-amused. "Have I ever told you that you're romantic? Geez. I want to be your boyfriend, even if you're terrible at compliments."

We kissed and Nancy cooed.

Chapter Twenty-One

I fumbled with Blake's shirt, got it loose, and ran my hands up his chest.

Blake was grabbing at my hair, and my shoulders, and everywhere he could find. His nails sunk into my back and pulled me closer. I grabbed his firm ass and pulled him closer as well, trying my best to press our chests together.

Blake gasped against my lips, eyelashes fluttering. "Oh, Jake—"

I let my hands wander to the front of his pants, rubbing just right where he wanted. I kissed up his neck and moaned when his back arched.

"Shit, Jake, I don't know—"

I pulled right off him. "Oh wow, sorry, that got heated."

Blake gave me a look that was somewhere in the middle between shy and turned on. "Yeah, that was really hot."

We were both in the front of my car. We'd been about to leave the restaurant parking lot, when Blake called me his boyfriend and said he'd had a great time, I'd gotten irrationally turned on by the word boyfriend, and then we'd leaned in for a quick kiss...that turned into a little more.

Geez. When Michaela said sex was on the table for us, I never thought I'd be hoping that she was right.

Blake looked so damn sexy with his hair all tangled from the way I'd been running my fingers from it. His eyes were a little glazed over from lust and his breath was coming rapidly.

"I'm sorry," I blurted, surprised by my own feelings of guilt. "That was probably way too fast for you considering you were straight only a few weeks ago—"

"Dude."

"I hope I didn't freak you out at all," I continued.

"Dude!" Blake snorted. "I was never straight. I just pretended like I was, which is kinda easy when you're bi. That was hot. I just don't wanna like...do stuff in a car."

At 11 am. In the bright parking lot of a relatively small breakfast place.

I was so dumb.

I cleared my throat. "Oh."

Maybe my Straight Blake™ worries hadn't completely gone away.

Blake rolled his eyes and kissed me again. "Wasn't it me, two seconds ago, who was low-key demanding sex? I'm obviously not going to freak out at a hot make out sesh."

"Hey, you're the guy going shit, Jake, I don't know—"

A blush spread over his cheeks, making me want to kiss them. Blake nibbled at his fingernail and shrugged. "Sorry. I guess I just overthought things a little. Man, we suck at being a couple already, huh?"

"No. Look, we're already openly communicating about our personal is-sues," I pointed out. "So far, we've passed all of my tests. There's simply no reason to pretend like we shouldn't be together. In a way, we're great for each other."

Blake was so sexy when he looked all blushy like that. "We really are."

We kissed.

Aw, we were just so stinking cute and precious. It almost stayed the way, until I saw a familiar rat heading our way.

Stupid Alana waved brightly and turned so that she was heading our way. My heart sunk in my chest.

"Have you ever done anything sexual with her?" I grumbled, watching Blake's face carefully.

Judging by Blake's expression, it was best that I didn't know. I already had it out for Alana anyway.

Stupid Alana knocked on the window and Blake rolled it down. "Hi, boys!" she chirped, because chirped was the only word to ever describe Stupid Alana's tone of voice. "Please tell me I'm not interrupting freaky car stuff."

I was not going to respond to this wart on the face of Blake's life.

Blake laughed awkwardly. "No, Alana, that would be weird."

Stupid Alana shrugged and gave him a meaningful look. "C'mon Blakey, it really wouldn't be your first time doing freaky car stuff. No need to act above it now to impress your new boyfriend."

Blake shot me a guilty look and I grimaced. I did not want to know at all. The thought of it was making me physically ill.

"I really don't feel comfortable hearing about straight people sex," I snapped. "It's not that I hate it, I just don't understand it, you know?"

Stupid Alana tipped her head back and laughed. It looked a little bit like any evil villain ever. "It's not straight people sex if we're both bi!"

She was bi too? And so was that Kelly girl? Was everyone on the face of the planet bi these days?

I was not happy with the idea that maybe Stupid Alana could connect with Blake in a way that I couldn't over something they both shared. This bitch had to go.

"Fine," I growled. "I'm uncomfortable with hearing about sex that involves you. Because you have a vagina and those repulse me. Please leave the car now."

Blake was facepalming, but hopefully not in an angry way. "Bye, Alana," he mumbled. "Sorry."

Stupid Alana got that stupid look on her face that suggested maybe she wasn't evil and I was a mean person. I hated that look. She lacked perspective.

But nonetheless, she waved a bit and I gladly rolled up the window before she'd even turned around.

"What kind of rude bitch," I snapped, "comes up to me talking about the sex life she had with MY boyfriend? What the hell. I do not want to know or care. She is infuriating."

"To be fair," Blake began, giving me a seriously judgmental look. "We've been boyfriends for all of twenty minutes. And a week ago you treated me like I was the actual plague. So."

"I thought you were a homophobe," I growled. "And she should know that you're pretty much spoken for, which is why I announced in front of the whole school that I want to go to prom with you. She's a rude bitch."

I got a nice shove in the shoulder from Blake. "Don't use that word. She's fine. You're being mean, Jake."

It hit me all at once.

"You're still in love with her," I said, leaning away from him and staring at him in shock.

Blake rolled his eyes so hard it looked like it should've given him a headache. "Oh my holy Jesus, Jake."

"There is not a single other explanation!"

He sighed. "Or you are extremely jealous of her because she's my ex, and you're into me. It could also be that simple, dude."

"You are the cockiest, slimiest, rudest, most awful—"

"I'll prove it to you!" Blake decided, looking at me with those sparkling green eyes. Ugh, he was always filled with such light and happiness. It confused me. "We'll hang out with Alana and you'll see that she isn't so bad."

Hang out? With a human?

"She's a great person I'm sure," I backtracked. "I really don't need first-hand knowledge. Or hanging out. Yeah, I'm actually good, I'll send her an apology letter in the—"

"We're doing it!"

Fucking hell. Blake the mistake was back at it again.

Chapter Twenty-Two

- -

"Okay, there are a few angles here," Christi said. We were all lounging in Ben's basement, watching Star Wars because apparently it was sinful that I hadn't seen it. "On one hand, you're sexist. On the other hand, you're petty and jealous. On the third, she's evil."

I nodded. "The truth is clear to me."

Kay sighed and leaned her head on Ben's shoulder. "It's kinda sad to know he's sexist. Everything else about him is fine."

"I'm not!"

Ben snapped his fingers and gave me a finger gun. "But you are! You called her a bitch for no reason, for one. For two, you're automatically assuming that because she's a female she's lusting after your man, because women are naturally—note the sarcasm—only motivated by the notion of sucking a man's cock. You also called her vagina repulsive."

"Not her vagina," I corrected. "All vaginas. Vaginas as a concept in general."

"See, that's actually worse."

"I'm gay."

Christi tossed her hair and sent Ben a meaningful look. She mouthed 'excuses'.

"Fine, whatever," I groaned. "Maybe I'm sexist or something. But I honestly think Stupid Alana is coming for my man—and I have to spend time with her today." I looked at the clock. "In two hours."

Kay grimaced. "Yeah, that's awk. Maybe Blake is introducing you guys so he can suggest a threesome later?"

I waited. No one spoke. "Oh, so you'll all call me sexist, but when Kay is obviously biphobic, we're all going to remain silent? Classy. Not all bisexuals are hoebags, Kay."

"Having a threesome doesn't make you a hoebag," Christi claimed, because Christi was a weird sex enthusiast on the low. "In fact, what's wrong with being a hoebag? Don't be boneheaded, Jake."

I groaned and leaned back on the couch. "You're not helping me. I need advice on what to do with Stupid Alana when I see her today. Kill her and hide her body? Tell her she's terrible and that Blake is all mine? Maybe Blake and I can make out in front of her for hours to get the point across."

"Maybe you could apologize for being a sexist pig."

"Kay!"

My friends sucked.

—//—

I was actually nervous to hang out with Alana. Not because she was intimidating, because Stupid Alana ain't shit, but because I was sort of thinking of it as a competition.

Was Blake putting us in the same room to see which one of us he liked better? Was he going to dump me and make sweet, non-stressful, heterosexual love to Alana right next to me? I would vomit.

"Stop making that angry face," Blake snapped. "We're doing this for you."

My brain made a record-scratch sound.

"For me?! You utter imbecile. I am not excited about this situation. In fact, I have an extremely rusty chainsaw in my shed out back. I would honestly rather start that chainsaw up and shove it right up my un-penetrated asshole than see Alana's stupid face right now."

Blake glared. "You're being annoying. Alana's cool. And yes, it is for you, because you'll now see that we're just friends and always will be."

Blake calling me annoying and Alana cool within the same breath made me very comfortable with this whole situation. Absolutely. This was grand.

"I simply am confused and baffled," I stressed to him, hoping he would understand from my tone how confused and baffled I was. "Because you claim that you had a crush on me when we were childhood friends, and that crush somehow lasted the test of time and remains to this day."

"You don't have to say that with such a tone."

"But! You dated Alana in the middle of this timeline," I noted. "She highjacked your emotions. Don't you think she wants to get you back?"

Blake looked annoyed, stared at me long enough to be awkward, and then melted. He sighed, shook his head, and took my hand. "You don't have to be worried, muscles. My emotions aren't being highjacked, okay?"

He leaned up onto his tiptoes, so I took the hint and leaned down to kiss him. "I don't like the way you're spinning this," I noted. "I do not care about your emotions or how they're being highjacked."

Blake was back to rolling his eyes. "You're the worst. I can't wait for the day you cry and tell me you love me."

Ew. That was a horrific thought. I felt a little nauseous. Emotions and vulnerability? Yucky.

"I know what you're thinking, and I think it's exhausting that you continue to be nervous about emotional vulnerability," Blake growled. He glared at me through tangled brown curls. "You're super annoying."

We pulled into the driveway and my heart sunk. Great. We were at the stupid house of Stupid Alana and I still had yet to convince Blake that I wasn't extremely annoying.

Alana answered the door in a pastel-colored maxi skirt and a shirt that looked like someone had chopped a rectangle off of a wedding dress and tied it around her boobs. Her hair fell in dark waves over her shoulders. Basically, and I was gay so I wasn't the best judge, but I was pretty sure she looked smoking fucking hot.

I watched Blake's face intently, but he met her eyes and grinned. "Thanks for doing this, 'Lana. I think you're really gonna like Jake."

'Lana?! She got a hippie nickname and I got muscles? Oh, and my favorite, dude? This was a horrific situation.

Alana grinned a smile wider than the Grand Canyon and hugged Blake. "I'm so excited!" She sent me a look over his shoulder, but I couldn't decode her expression. "You guys are such a cute couple, by the way."

Ugh. What a snake.

When it was clear that all I was going to do was glare, Blake smiled and said, "thanks" bashfully. Then he kicked my ankle as she led us into her kitchen, because he was secretly a monster.

But fine. I could be polite. "Nice house," I said.

Alana's smile looked super uncomfortable. "Thanks, Jake."

There. That was very peaceful and agreeable. Could I go home now?

It struck me that I definitely was into Blake Beckson. Like, soon to be in love with Blake Beckson. Because if it wasn't that, why on earth was I putting up with this situation?

"So, we're going to bake cookies, right?" Blake asked, all happy-like. "What kind do you want to make, Alana?"

Right, because Jake's opinion on cookies was total shit. Who cared about the cookies Jake liked? Fuck Jake.

I was slightly bothered.

Then it got a million times worse.

Blake smiled and rolled his eyes in a playful manner, and said, "Let me guess, sugar cookies. Again."

Alana beamed and smacked Blake's stomach with the bag of mix she had on the table. "Don't crap on sugar cookies! They're like the greatest in the entire world."

"Where's your bathroom?" I asked. Alana pointed me towards the hallway so I left to go sulk in the bathroom.

I did not want to be around cute straight couple Alana and Blake. I didn't want to think that Alana and Blake used to make sugar cookies all the time when they were together, and they were walking down memory lane or something.

I texted Ben. This sucks, I said. They're like totally in love.

Ben texted back words of wisdom. You're always so dramatic.

You're subtle homophobic comments don't make people think you're straight, I responded.

Ben: ???!!?

I ignored him and decided I'd sulked for about the length of time someone would pee.

I walked out of the bathroom to Blake, with his arms crossed. "You didn't flush," he snapped. "I've been standing outside of this door the whole time and you never flushed."

I waved my hand at the toilet. "Do you want to inspect it?"

Blake grimaced. "That sounds like the line a bully would pull on a middle schooler before a swirly. Stop avoiding Alana, man. She's really trying to be nice and you're making things awkward."

I glared at Blake. "Has anyone told you that you're the height of a middle schooler? That's awkward."

I walked away from him. He followed behind, grumbling about cheap insults and pettiness.

Alana was waiting for us in the kitchen with a mixer and bowls, and all the ingredients. Yay. Less time we'd have to spend doing dumb cookies.

"Okay, are we ready?" cookie drill sergeant Alana said. "Jake, you can mix together the liquids. I'll do the solids. And then it's always Blake's job to mix them all together, huh?" She smiled at him.

Great. Now Alana thought she was queen of the cookies, and they apparently had a designated cookie process because they were just so stinking cute.

I was in hell.

Chapter Twenty-Three

It was after the cookies were in the oven (ten more minutes until we could leave!) and Blake was in the bathroom, that things finally got real.

Alana leaned in and glared, the first time she hadn't acted all polite and kind and above-it-all. "I know why you're such an asshole to me," she snapped.

"Because you're trying to steal my man?" I questioned.

She rolled her eyes. "No."

Huh, maybe I was a sexist.

"Because I will steal your man," Alana growled.

Oh good, I wasn't sexist. Alana was just a cliché.

"You do realize that your behavior kind of ruins the reputation of women everywhere, right?" I asked. "It's kind of an embarrassment."

Alana rolled her eyes. "I don't care about all women and the weird things you say. I care about the fact that when Blake dumped me he told me that he liked someone else. And that someone was you. You literally destroyed—"

"Right," I agreed. "That was harsh of him. So why aren't you mad at him? Or why don't you choose to date someone who's actually going to choose you first and treat you right? You're acting like how women act in movies that men write."

Alana faltered a little. Then she resumed track. "I would usually agree." Well, at least that was something. "But this time isn't the case. Blake doesn't actually like you, he's just confused because you've spent this whole time acting like he's the worst, and he's finally won you over. He probably feels like you're more important than—"

"Are the cookies done yet?" Blake asked, because Blake was a magician who totally teleported to and from that bathroom.

"Were you in the bathroom for ten minutes?" I asked with some snark, angry because Blake didn't believe me and my friends didn't believe me and Alana was actually evil. "No? Then they aren't done."

Usually I was rude, but apparently that was more rude than usual. Blake blinked. "Are you okay?"

"Dandy," I sighed. "Your friend is being a lovely host."

Blake looked at me like I was being weird, but didn't care too much. "Okay, well let's like watch TV or something while we wait."

I tossed myself in an armchair and gave Oblivious and his girlfriend the couch. Blake gave me another weird look but I stared at the TV and ignored him. He was annoying.

After awkward TV watching and cookies that tasted like betrayal and gross inside jokes between Blake and his ex, I finally escaped.

"So," Blake said after we'd gotten into the car. "Maybe that was a really bad idea."

"That sucked."

"Drive slow," Blake said. "We need to talk."

It was constant emotional vulnerability with this guy.

"She just told me she wants to get back together with you," I ratted her out. I saw no reason not to. "Like I thought. So actually, I'm not sexist or annoying."

"Really?!" Blake made a face. "You got lucky."

"I could tell," I denied. "The way she looks at you. The way she flaunted weird inside jokes from your past. She laughs at your jokes and you're rarely funny. She—"

"Jake!" Blake protested. "I'm hilarious, dude, first of all, so shut up. But... yeah. Yeah, I get what you're saying. I'm sorry, man, I didn't know. Sorry for pushing it. I knew Alana liked me, but we had a talk yesterday about how we were gonna stay friends and stuff."

I found myself wanting to be bitter, but unable to be. Blake saw the best in his friend and didn't assume that she had manipulative intentions. There really was nothing wrong with that.

I turned to him, keeping an eye on the road. "You guys were friends though, weren't you? You really gelled."

Blake fidgeted awkwardly. "I don't like the way you sound, dude. Yeah, we knew each other pretty well. But we can bake cookies together and shit, Jake. We have time."

For whatever reason, Blake's promise to bake cookies together and shit was reassuring. "I felt like you obviously should be with her," I admitted, because this was emotional vulnerability time. "Because of all your jokes and stuff."

Blake smacked my arm and then shook his hand in pain, which was pretty flattering. "Idiot. We have jokes, maybe."

We both silently absorbed the fact that we had no jokes.

"Well, we don't have jokes because of your deadpan personality," Blake said, but there was an upturn to his mouth and his eyes were bright, so maybe he wasn't head over ugly sneakers for Stupid Alana.

"I am secretly very funny," I protested. "Ben laughs at me all the time. I mean with me. Of course."

Blake laughed just as we pulled into his driveway. I turned to him and kissed him. I kissed him until he was grinning, and then I pressed kisses up his neck so that his grin turned to a gasp.

We pulled away and I kept my hand in his hair, ready to kiss him again at any moment. His smile faded into an expression that was a lot more serious, which was maybe what spurred me to say what I said next.

"It scared me," I admitted. "The thought of you leaving me and going back to Stupid Alana. I hated thinking that it could happen. I don't really know when it happened, or how, but I really like you Blake the snake."

Blake's hand reached up to grab my forearm and his thumb stroked the skin there, giving me goosebumps. He turned his head a little and kissed the inside of my wrist. "I would never leave you, Jake the unfathomably rude asshole."

I laughed and he kissed me. I soaked in the terrible relief I felt at just hearing the words leave his mouth. I was attached to him so much that I would push around timid gay kids to take him to prom, or put up with vivacious exes so that he wouldn't be grumpy.

"I'm starting to worry that there's nothing I won't do for you," I snorted.

Blake rolled his eyes. "I can reassure you. Hey Jake, want to work on our project? It's an essay and we have two days left to do it and we've accomplished nothing."

"What fucking project?" I blurted, utterly confused.

Blake looked deadpan. "Yeah, that's what I thought. You're such a jock. I actually hate you. Not enough to go back to my ex, but definitely enough to take the rest of your leftover cookies."

Because Blake the mistake was total evil and vile, he grabbed the Tupperware container of cookies that was in my backseat and waved it in my face. I kissed him again, and we got caught up in each other.

I wanted to lock the doors and talk to him until it was midnight and my mom was calling me to make sure I wasn't murdered. I wanted to hear every dumb thing his dumb mouth could say, and I wanted to make fun of him until he hit my arm like he had before. I wanted to hear him insult me and ask about my friends. I wanted to talk about his friends, and I hated learning things about people.

Blake pulled away, eyelashes lowered and lips red from kissing. "I should go."

Please don't.

"Yeah," I gasped. "Meet you at the mailbox tomorrow?"

He smiled. I had never believed that hearts could quicken, or skip a beat, or any of that gooey romantic garbage, but when Blake smiled my heart did all of those things. Hell, when Blake Beckson smiled my heart danced the fucking foxtrot.

"Yeah."

Fuck. Fuck. When did this happen? I was left waiting until he got inside safe, and then waved at his mom through the window. I was obsessed.

I went to bed that night, heart still beating fast.

Chapter Twenty-Four

Blake and I finished our project the next day. We basically wrote paragraphs in between each of our classes, desperately trying to get something on the paper. Blake thought our essay sucked.

He kept looking at it in dismay. "Shit, this is due tomorrow. It's the worst thing I've ever written."

I leaned over his shoulder. "I think this actually might be the best thing I've ever written. I can't believe we met the page requirement. I always thought that was more of a suggestion."

Blake groaned and dropped his head into his hands. "Jake, dude. You're amazing, I am super into you and all, but you're actually the worst partner ever."

"You're evil. I gave it my best effort. You're just judgmental, Beckson."

"Guys!" a random girl said, skipping on up to me and Blake. What was her name again? Melissa? Morgan?

"Hey, Michaela," Blake said, looking a little awkward.

Riiight. This was the girl who asked bluntly about our sex lives.

"So!" She clapped her hands. "Here's my idea. I'm thinking what we're going to do is add a third box when voting for prom king or queen that says 'Jake and Blake.' It's only fair that you guys get a shot."

"Prom is months away," I sighed, wishing this girl wasn't so obsessed with our relationship.

"I'm just saying!" Michaela exclaimed. "If they try to move the box we can post about it on the internet and say it's a hate crime. Then one of you could sue the school for millions of dollars."

I perked up. "I'm broke and I'm listening."

Blake smacked my stomach. "Chill out, asshole. We're not suing the school for millions of dollars."

I sulked.

"Besides, the fall ball is coming up—"

"The what?" I snorted. "The fall ball? That is the dumbest, least creative name I have ever heard."

Blake poked my stomach. "Dude, don't be annoying. It's the most recent dance. There's the fall ball, the snowball, the spring fling, then prom. Didn't you know that?"

I was too busy snickering at the horrible names our school came up with to respond. Blake rolled his eyes.

"And since you're my boyfriend now, we're going to all of them together," Blake declared, looking determined. My laughter died in a second.

"Aw!" Michaela squealed. "You guys are such icons."

I hated Michaela more and more each day.

"I'd rather break up with Blake than go to the stupid fall ball," I growled. "Sorry if that ruins your gay fangirl dreams."

Blake actually looked a little sad about missing out on the dances, which really shouldn't have shocked me. If I hadn't learned already from his ugly joggers and vans, Blake liked to follow the crowd and do cringy things.

Michaela's jaw dropped. "Wait," she said in a very loud voice. "You're telling me, Blake will have nobody to go with to fall ball?"

I was super confused until I noticed greasy Gabe right across the hallway perk up his greasy tail and grin a greasy grin.

"No!" I yelled. "I was kidding, obviously I'm taking Blake to fall ball. Jesus, what's with all the weird school dances I'm committing to?"

Gabe greasily frowned and went back to minding his business. I glared, just in case he decided to pay attention to my boyfriend one more time. Michaela winked at Blake and walked away.

Blake patted my shoulder. "You really don't have to worry about Gabe. Obviously. I don't want to make you go to the fall ball if you aren't interested in going. I know you're still, I don't know, embarrassed?"

I tugged off my sweatshirt and shoved it at Blake. "Remember the day you wore my sweatshirt to school?"

His deadpan look proved that, after approximately a day of dating, he was already sick of my shit. "Are you avoiding emotional vulnerability by trying to change the topic?"

He was useless. I began to wrestle the sweatshirt over his head. "Wear this. So slimy, GREASY, GAYS realize that you're MINE."

Gabe looked over and hurried away. Good riddance.

"Keep walking, Gabe!" I yelled after him.

Gabe tripped, dropped a book, looked back and realized it wasn't worth stopping, and broke into a jog.

By the time my boyfriend appeared again, he was wearing my sweatshirt and his hair was floofed from static electricity. He was also glaring. "Did you know," he began testily. "That you have a very difficulty personality?"

I straightened my sweatshirt over his shoulders and kissed his forehead. "There we go," I decided. "Now he'll stay away."

The forehead kiss did not soothe my boyfriend's angry scowl. "You're also a bully," he continued. "You owe Gabe an apology. Or, like, twelve apologies."

"He needs to stop drooling after you," I growled, wrapping my arms around my boyfriend and kissing his temple. "You're obviously taken. We're going to do that stupid box idea too, so greasy and trombone don't win prom king and king."

"You're an awful person, dude. I hate you, low-key."

We obviously had a very normal and functional relationship.

I ruffled his hair and scanned the hallways for treacherous sluts like Alana and Gabe. "When is this ball again? I need to prepare for socialization about a week in advance."

"It's tomorrow, dipshit."

"On a Tuesday?!"

"Bruh," Blake sighed, turning his baseball cap backwards in typical straight boy fashion. He was also wearing very baggy jeans and a shirt with pickles on it and, which I took to be some sort of declaration that he liked penis.

"Get over it. It's a dumb little dance. Let's just go, hang out with friends, maybe dance together?"

I had never been to a school dance before. Did people get drunk? Did Blake do that white person thing where he kept his feet in place and bounced his knees? I did not really want to know.

"Okay, so here's the plan," Blake said, and those were beginning to be my least favorite words. "We should totally wear bi and gay themed shirts."

I did not want to do that. "No way in hell," I growled.

Blake grabbed my hands and I felt a spark of affection. He gave me puppy dog eyes, big green eyes looking sweet and innocent. His kissable mouth wobbled. My heart completely melted. "Please?"

"Fine," I growled.

Blake's eyes lit up. "You are starry-eyed! That's so hot. You're awesome. I like you. Time for class."

With one last quick kiss on the cheek, my boyfriend scampered away from me, leaving me with my cheeks fuming.

Chapter Twenty-Five

I pouted. I was wearing a shirt with black and white light sabors lined up on the bottom, each shooting a different color of the pride flag. Blake was in a shirt that had a glass of white wine and a glass of red, with text that said "I'm into both."

He'd already been spoken to by two teachers about not wearing alcohol-related paraphernalia.

They were very stupid people.

Ben was break dancing in the middle of a circle. He was that kid at school.

Gabe and Kevin were standing face-to-face, keeping their feet planted and bouncing their knees. I glared at them to exert my dominance as the better gay couple at school. Blake tugged me away and placed his hands on my shoulders.

"Don't glare at them," he scolded. "Let them live their lives."

I let my hands drop to Blake's waist and we swayed back and forth a little, even though the music was quick and electronic. "Are we practicing for prom?"

Blake's smile made my heart skip a beat. "Yeah. And at prom, we're gonna be the best couple there."

"So you admit that it's a competition?"

"Okay, I'm done talking. Sway romantically or else."

I let my fingers run through his curly brown mop of hair, affectionately tugging a little bit. I didn't even realize that I was smiling at him until Blake was smiling back, practically radiating sunshine and happiness.

I was falling in love with him.

I was almost certain that was the truth. I hung on Blake's every word, constantly wanted to be with him, and needed to be as close to him as possible.

I opened my mouth to share my secret, when—

"Jaaaake!" Ben yelled, grabbing my arm. "Can you believe that I helped get you guys together? I love you both so much!"

Ben apparently also loved beating me to declarations of love.

"Ben," I growled. "Yes, I love you too. I have something I think I need to say to Blake, though, and you'd gladly support—"

"No, not yet!" Ben yelped. "Kay and Christi and I need you for a slight minute. Some drama llama is happening."

I tried not to roll my eyes and grimaced at the boy I loved. "I'll be right back. Don't go too far!"

Blake was laughing, though, so all hope wasn't lost.

I let Ben tug me away, feeling lightheaded and elated. I loved Blake. I needed to tell him! I was going to tell him, and maybe even he would love me back.

I looked back, for once last glance of my boyfriend, only to find him standing next to Alana, frowning.

I put on the brakes. "Ben! Wait!"

Ben tugged, and shit he was strong for a short kid. "No time for waiting, hunk! There's shit happening right now, I just got some juicy texts."

Yeah, the shit happening was the fact that Alana was probably about to drug my boyfriend and kidnap him.

I turned back to Ben, all elation gone. I had to trust Blake to stay away from the conniving jerk face. That was the whole point of being in love, or in a relationship. Trust. Problem-solving. Good communication. Blake and I had practiced those things!

"What's going on?" I asked Ben, hoping to get this over as quickly as possible.

"Some guys from Richmond are here," Ben whispered, as if I was supposed to know what that meant. At my blank stare, he rolled his eyes. "You know how our high school is filled with dweebs and nerds and happy people? Richmond is filled with assholes who like to kick ass. Christi's cousin is one of them and she's not happy."

A little concerned for Christi's safety now, I caught up with Ben and we went to the front of the school. Most of the teachers were gone at this point, off fucking each other or taking shots in the bathroom or something.

Christi was screaming in the face of a jacked guy, almost as big as me. "—and you have no right to come here and ruin everything!" she finished.

"Okay, you're big and scary," Ben explained, giving me a little shove. "Make them leave."

I approached Christi and she looked relieved to see me. "Jake! This asshole is Ross. He's my cousin. His friends shouldn't be here, they're only here to start trouble and I know it. A few of them went down the hall."

I crossed my arms and stepped in front of Christi. "What the fuck are you doing here?" I growled at Ross.

Ross was kind of scrubby and gross, with greasy black facial hair and sunken brown eyes. He kind of looked like he rolled out of a garbage can recently. "I'm here for a friend," he said, voice not nearly as intimidating as I was expecting. "Not to start trouble."

Christi snorted. "Fuck yourself. Jake, he's an asshole. He told my whole family about my sexuality without my permission. He hasn't said a nice thing to me since. I don't want him here."

There were a group of people from my school gathered around, looking curious about the commotion. I wasn't sure why Christi's experience with her cousin made him a bad person who was here to start trouble, rather than a bad person who just wanted to come to a dance.

But, ya know, I trusted her judgment.

I took a step forward, allowing my muscles to flex. "You're going to have to get the hell out of here, or we'll have trouble."

Usually people backed off without bothering to figure out if there was any bite behind my bark. Not Ross. His gaze darted down, and then he smirked. "Have you looked in the fucking mirror to see what you're wearing? I'm really not scared of a faggot."

I grinned. "Oh, you really should be."

I grabbed the front of Ross' shirt and shoved him backwards so far he landed on his tailbone. He gritted his teeth and shot up from the ground, only to swing at me. I stepped back and laughed a little when he punched the air in front of me. His face reddened in rage.

"What the fuck ever," he spat. "Jaron is taking care of Alana's shit anyway."

Alana?

The name shocked me still and Ross took advantage, swinging his fist again and grazing my jaw. I stumbled back and turned around, looking down the hallway that Christi had gestured towards.

"Christi..." I mumbled. "There's more of them?"

Ben jumped in front of me and faced off with Ross. "I'll stop him! If you think they're pulling some dumb shit, go after them!"

Which would have been very sweet, except Ross doubled over laughing. "Your Oompa Loompa ass is going to stop me?"

I grimaced. Ben did not like being called short.

Ben's face twisted in anger. "Excuse me?" he swung his leg and kicked Ross in the balls, causing Ross to drop like a ton of bricks.

I paused to snicker, then remembered the situation. "Thanks, Ben!" I ran down the hallway.

What the hell was Alana up to?

Chapter Twenty-Six

I found the group of men in one of the classrooms. I didn't know what to expect. Part of me was expecting them to have pinned Blake down and beat the shit out of him. Another part of me was picturing Alana gleefully giggling as Blake bled out on the floor.

I had thought the whole situation over so many times in my head that I was already seething with rage by the time I reach the classroom.

Instead, the scene before me was completely bizarre.

"What...is going on?" I asked, sharing at the room of people.

Two guys had Blake by each arm, keeping him firmly in place. Rather than struggle, Blake was glaring at everybody, looking kind of bored. Alana was embracing another one of the guys in a passionate kiss.

My jaw dropped. "Uh...Alana?"

Blake shook his head and looked at me in defeat. "I thought they were gonna beat me up, dude," he admitted. "But they actually just wanted to keep me in place while making out with Alana."

"Odd fetish," I mused.

Alana turned on me and shoved her finger at the door. "Leave, asshole!"

"Okay." I turned around.

"Jake, what the fuck?" Blake called after me.

I turned back and sighed."Fine, I'll stay." I looked at the weirdness in front of me. Usually I would try to come up with some sort of sarcastic remark, but I was too shocked to even bother. "What are you doing?"

Alana shrugged and gestured at the people from Richmond. "I'm making Blake jealous."

My head hurt. I gave Blake a defeated look. "Well... have fun then." I turned to leave.

"You are joking!" Blake yelled. "That is not funny, dumbass!"

I turned on my heel and rolled my eyes. "Do you now see that your ex-girlfriend is crazy? She is literally making out with a ton of guys in front of you so you'll turn straight again."

Alana scoffed. "He is straight. You're just confusing him."

"Oh!" I gasped. "There we go! It doesn't matter if I had some originally sexist thoughts about you, because you're clearly homophobic."

One of the guys stepped away from Alana and wrinkled his nose. "You're homophobic? That's fucked, man."

The hypocrisy. I glared. "You should know that your friend Ross is also homophobic. He called me a fag."

The guy's frown deepened.

Alana rolled her eyes. "I am not homophobic. This asshole spent time at my boyfriend's house, convinced him he was gay, and my boyfriend broke up with me to date him."

Dude bro shrugged. "Well that's pretty fucked too, man."

Blake groaned. "Okay, I probably shouldn't have broke up with you by saying I was into a guy. And now that I think about it, it was probably kind of misleading of me to say that I just needed a break to try out something new." I facepalmed. "And I shouldn't have said I would get back together with you if it didn't work out. And that one time I said it felt like it was possibly a phase is starting to seem like a poor choice—"

"You brought this onto yourself," I grumbled. "Good luck."

"Jake!" Blake whined. "Don't leave!"

I rolled my eyes. "Now I don't even blame her. Are you stupid?"

"I was just letting her down easy," Blake insisted. "And, to be fair, I didn't know if this whole thing with you was gonna work out! But it did, Alana."

Something shifted in Alana's expression. "So you're telling me you're actually never getting back together with me?"

I sighed. "Finally, she gets it. Like a week later than most people would, but some are slower than others."

"Exactly, Alana," Blake stressed. "Jake and I are happy."

Her eyes narrowed. "Okay then, fine. Guys, now you can beat him up."

Dude bro hesitated. "I mean, I'm kind of thinking that's an overreaction—"

"Chad!" One of the guys holding Blake yelled. "She's paying us each a hundred dollars. Beat the kid up."

Chad gave me weird side-eye, like he was uncertain for a moment, and then he glanced down at my shirt. With a moment of resolution, he turned and swung his fist at Blake's face.

I was halfway across the room before I'd consciously decided to move, and my vision tunneled in on Chad hitting Blake in the face. Blake's head snapped to the side and blood gushed from his mouth. Rage gripped me more harshly than it ever had in my entire life.

I bodied Chad out of the way and grabbed one of the guys holding Blake back. He had just enough time to say, "Oh, shi—" before I'd slammed my fist into his gut.

I turned around fast enough to watch Blake weasel his way out of the other guy's grip. He ran to me and I took him up into my arms. "We've gotta get out of here—" Blake gasped.

"I love you," I blurted.

Blake's jaw dropped and his eyes went wide. His expression combined with blood gushing down his face wasn't the most attractive thing in the world, and yet I still wanted to kiss him until he was breathless. Yup, I loved him.

"Really?" Blake asked.

Alana growled. "You two are fucking disgusting. Chad! Jaron! What the hell?"

Chad was sprawled on the ground, groaning about his tailbone. His friend was hunched over, trying to catch his breath. The other guy looked at the ceiling, obviously trying to pretend like he was invisible.

"That's three hundred dollars going right back into my bank account," Alana snapped. Like it was some sort of magic word, the guys were back on their feet.

"C'mon!" Blake yelped, tugging me out of the room. We made a break for it, rushing down the hallway with three giant guys hustling after us. "I can run a five minute mile," Blake gasped. "So I hope you can keep up with that."

"I run sprints for the track team." I gave him a smirk. "I'm holding back right now."

"Then let's move!"

We hauled ass towards the main entrance, where Ben was still screaming in Ross' face. Ross was sprawled on the ground, protectively covering his crotch. "Bye, guys!" I yelled as we burst through the front door.

"Holy shi—" Ben exclaimed at what was probably our pursuers.

"Prom better not have this much drama," I growled under my breath. Blake looked over and nodded, eyes wide and mouth gasping for air.

We managed to haul ass all the way to our homes, not bothering to look back. Blake grabbed my arm and directed me to his backyard, which had a swings leftover from his childhood days. We landed on our knees underneath the slide, gasping and laughing.

"We did it—" I gasped for air and ruffled Blake's hair. It was plastered to his forehead with sweat. "Shit— your face."

Blake's hand went to his nose. It came away red and his eyes widened. "Holy shit. You don't think they made it here, right?"

We poked our heads out from under the slide and inspected the backyard. It was hard to see through the darkness of the night, but it seemed empty.

Blake and I exchanged a victorious grin, and then we were kissing.

Chapter Twenty-Seven

We snuck into Blake's house through the back way and made our way to his bedroom. I could hear his parents watching TV in the room over, so I made sure to keep my voice down.

"Ow!" Blake exclaimed. "You are such an asshole."

"Sh," I said, prodding his nose with my fingers. "I don't think it's broken, but shouldn't we get you to the hospital or something?"

"No," he scoffed. "I'm fine, we just have to clean up the blood a little and I'll be good as new."

"Fine— here." I grabbed a pair of boxer shorts off of the ground and Blake stumbled away. "Come back, we have to clean you."

"Dude!" Blake sputtered and held his hands up to keep me away. "Dude, you do not want to know the fluids on that thing. Hold on, I'll go to the bathroom."

"Nope." I steadied my hands on his shoulders and kept him sitting on the bed. "You're staying here. You're injured."

"Wha—"

I left the room and slinked off towards the bathroom, making sure my feet were quiet enough that his parents wouldn't notice. I grabbed a small dish towel and ran it under the water, then rummaged through his cabinets for a first aid kid.

I entered Blake's bedroom and halted, shocked to see him smiling. "Thanks, jerk face," Blake said, holding out his hand. I knocked his hand away and started cleaning his face with the towel. "You're so bossy."

"Well, I have to be," I scoffed. "You're the one that got yourself into this mess—"

"You got punched too! I can see the bruise on your jaw."

I shook my head and wiped away the blood, little by little. "Not as bad as you," I scolded. "I can't believe you trusted Alana and followed her, idiot. You seriously could've been hurt."

Blake rolled his eyes. "She said she wanted to talk about something important. Not that she wanted to jump me with three meat-heads."

"Mhmm." I finished wiping all the blood off, and then I covered my finger with Neosporin and shoved it up Blake's nose.

"Dude!" Blake sputtered and wiped at his face, but I grabbed his hands in mine and sent him a stern glare.

"Blake. What if it gets infected?"

"You are so stupid!" Blake whined. "I don't have a cut, so it can't get infected. He hit my cheek and a little of my nose, man, I'm fine."

Huh. That was a very good point. "Oops," I mumbled, which made Blake smirk and shake his head a little.

He grabbed the tissue and blew his nose, getting blood and goop all over the towel. I got a lovely up-close view of Blake shoving a corner of the towel into each nostril to scoop out the shit that was up there. It was disgusting.

And yet, I still wanted to scoop him up in my arms and cuddle on him. And then I wanted to go find Chad and beat his face in. So yeah, I loved him.

...And he never said it back.

I awkwardly stared at Blake, trying to figure him out. He honestly was kind of a mess— hair sweaty and sticking to his forehead, cheek swollen and looking a little purple, nose covered in blood remnants and Neosporin. But his green eyes were as captivating as ever and I wanted to kiss his pretty lips.

He wasn't looking at me with the uncomfortable look of someone who didn't love the person who loved him. He also wasn't looking at me like he wanted to punch me in the face. But he also wasn't looking at me like he wanted to start confessing his love. Actually, he looked confused.

"Are you good?" Blake asked. He reached out and felt my forehead. "No fever. You look like you're about to pass out."

My heart hammered in my chest. I knew what I had to do.

Blake must've been running on adrenaline earlier. He must not have comprehended what I'd said. I'd have to say it all over again.

"Um." I wiggled. I felt awkward and too-large, like I wanted to melt into the blankets and hide. "Well." Was I blushing? "Um. I like your hair."

Blake blinked. "Did they drug you?"

"No! And your eyes; I think they're very pretty. Sorry, I'm not poetic." I cleared my throat. "And, um, I find your personality to be very enjoyable to be around. In fact, when given the opportunity to hang out with other people, I think I'd rather be with you."

Blake tilted his head, looking like he might've been putting together what I was saying.

"And I think we're very compatible," I added, looking at his eyes for any sign of disagreement. There wasn't any. "And if you would like to continue dating, I would very much like that. For a very long time."

Blake leaned in, smirking. "Oh? How long?"

"Like, as in, as long as you'd like."

"But if you could choose."

Blake Beckson was evil and I hated him.

"I think I'm blushing and I'm very embarrassed," I mumbled, staring at the carpet. Blake laughed.

"Oh, dude, you're totally blushing." He leaned back on the bed and grinned at me. "C'mon, I wanna hear you say it. I wanna watch you look at me and say it."

"You're the worst," I groaned, hiding my face in my hands. "Forever, maybe?"

Blake sat up and leaned against me, smiling in a way that lit up his whole face. "You know, Jake, I think I missed something you said earlier. Didn't I?" He wrapped his arm around mine and clasped my hand.

"Possibly," I admitted, taking a deep breath. "Blake—"

"Say those things you used to call me."

I groaned. "Blake the mistake—"

"That's more like it."

I grabbed his chin and met those electric green eyes, finding the courage to tell the man I loved what I had on my mind "I love you, Blake. Okay? I love you, and I've only just realized it."

Blake smiled so wide I thought his swollen cheek must've been hurting. Those eyes I used to pretend to hate were twinkling with delight— actually, he might've been crying a little. What a cute loser.

"Me too," he blurted, leaning his face against my shoulder. "I've actually liked you for kind of a long time, Jake. And now I get to tell you that I love you."

We kissed and I realized that, all along, I was the idiot. Blake was incredible, and I couldn't think of anything better than loving him.

-/-/-